*Now that they have reconnected,
will they make it out alive?*

THE

STORM

WE

BREATHE

A ROMANTIC SUSPENSE

ELAINE EVANS

To my husband.
For being the storm I breathe.

Also by

Elaine Evans

- Becoming Mallory

- All In

- His Last Shot

Author Note

Even though this is a romance and promises a happily-ever-after, this story contains elements common to romantic suspense that may be distressing for some readers. Please be aware that the book includes depictions of fire, the death of a parent both on and off the page, themes of stalking and kidnapping, and scenes in which characters are placed in serious peril.

I want you to enjoy your reading experience, so if any of these subjects are upsetting for you, please take care of yourself and read at your own comfort level.

The Storm We Breathe

Elaine Evans

Prologue

Three Days Prior

Diane

R unning in high heels is hard.

Running in stilettos? Even harder.

Add an evening gown, and you have yourself a real situation.

But I have no choice, because there's a madman chasing me through this parking garage.

Somewhere behind me, the stomp of boots on concrete echoes like a countdown. The distant city noise hums along with people living their lives. But down here, a damp danger clings to me. Plus, there's this throbbing pain in my feet, a constant reminder of my ill-fitting shoes. Each step is fire.

It's past eleven p.m., and the buzz of the fluorescent lights overhead is doing nothing but add to my already frazzled nerves. As I struggle to run, my body shakes uncontrollably, and I can't seem to gain any speed. Granted, I used to run marathons for fun, but now, as a fifty-four-year-old woman, I'm missing the fast pace of my youth. Adrenaline courses through me while I hold my clutch like a security blanket. The fiery sensation in my legs intensifies with each step as I focus on not twisting my ankle.

SNAP!

I tumble forward, face-planting onto the hard ground. Damnit! The heel of my shoe broke.

Why didn't I go with the cute ballet flats I originally planned on wearing? Then again, how was I supposed to know I'd be chased tonight? A scenario that you only have nightmares about.

But what is happening right now is all too real.

Sweat beads roll down my back, chafing against the scratchy material of my dress. With heavy, labored breaths, I tip my chin over my shoulder. I don't see him, so I crawl forward, propping myself up against a concrete pillar, whipping off my strappy heels and trying to catch my breath.

"Diane." My name on his tongue, cunning yet playful, pierces through the calm.

I freeze.

He's close, but I don't know where.

"Come out, come out, wherever you are." *Is this a game to him?*

Crawling across the dirty ground, I crouch between two SUVs, my back pressed to the metal, heart slamming like it wants to be released. A sharp pain pierces my arch as I dig my feet into the ground, trying to adjust. My hand flies to my mouth, desperate to contain the scream bubbling up.

Something's sliced the bottom of my foot.

Crimson red blood cascades down, landing on the piece of glass responsible. It's okay for now. But my chances of outrunning this lunatic now dropped a few percentage points.

Great.

Resting my head against the SUV's black car door, I peek at the rear-view mirror. Like a lion stalking its prey, he approaches. Menacing, dressed in all black, with a hoodie covering his face.

A ski mask included to make him even scarier.

I'm out of time.

And trapped.

I bite down on the urge to holler for help and attempt to steady my rigid breathing. Water dripping from a pipe nearby only heightens my anxiety.

"I can smell you, Diane." *God, he's creepy.*

Rose!

Immediately, my lovely, strong, and capable daughter's face flashes in my mind. I have no idea how this is going to end. But my gut is telling me … not well.

She has to know.

I dropped and shattered my phone while running, attempting to call 911, so I have only one option. Unclasping my clutch, I peer inside, searching for my small spiral notebook and pen. Something I always carry with me since mathematical equations swirl around in my brain 24/7. And thanks to the gift of aging, I'm more prone to forgetting when one comes to mind.

But now, I need this handy-dandy notebook for a very different reason.

I click the pen, flip open to the first page, and write.

To whomever finds this, please give it to the police.
Rose,
Tell

"There is nowhere for you to hide. I can hear your breathing." He's not panting or out of breath from the chase. Just … close. So close.

Frantically, my fingers grip the pen as I finish what may be my last thoughts and words to my baby girl. My world plummets as a sudden, unwelcome realization settles in.

I'll never see her find a good man.

Or watch her fall in love.

Get married.

Start a family.

A single tear tracks down my cheek while I write the last word. It's not what I wanted to say, but I pray it's enough.

With slow, determined movements, I rip the small white-lined paper from the metal spirals and fold it in half. Shifting, I slip the paper in the crack of the SUV's two doors. It's sticking out, visible against the shiny black paint job. Which hopefully will be enough for the driver of this vehicle to see it. If nothing else, it will fall out when they open their door.

I toss my clutch in front of the tire. It's all inside. ID, wallet, my late husband's wedding ring that I always carry with me. When the driver leaves, it will still be here, intact, ready to be found. At least the authorities can identify me.

And so will Rose.

My hand falls to the pavement. Wiggling my toes, I realize my foot is numb. Running is no longer an option. If this is the end, I'm going down swinging. Standing will expose me, but I'd rather he discovered me upright than lying on the floor.

I hold my breath, get my bearings, and grip the handle of the car door, pulling myself up.

This could be my last breath.

"There she is."

I scream.

Everything goes black.

Chapter One
5:25 p.m.
Three Days Later

Rose

Mom's been gone for three days.

And I miss her.

So much.

It's almost evening on a Monday, and I'm lying on my bed, holding my phone, waiting for my cousin Maggie to call me. My black Pomeranian Juno is curled up at my feet.

I've barely slept, and I'm not eating. I can't. Not until I know where my mom is.

The blades of the ceiling fan above me spin and spin as I stare at it, waiting.

I'm waiting for so much these days. It's ridiculous.

Waiting to hear from my editor about my next book. I submitted it to her before my life went to hell.

Waiting to hear any word from the detective about my mom.

Waiting for Maggie to call from Italy.

Lots and lots of waiting.

At this stage in my life, I never imagined this would be my reality. That my mom would vanish without a trace while attending a ball as a keynote speaker for the conference she was attending.

Sighing at the thought, I rub Juno's fur with my toes to quell my anxiety. The black fur ball's eyes shoot up at the contact. He loves it when I rub his head. It doesn't matter if it's with my toes or fingers, so he leans into the touch.

The familiar booping chirp of Facetime breaks me from my thoughts.

I lift my phone. It's Maggie.

Filling my lungs with the circulating air of the fan, I exhale it out and steady myself. I have to break the news to my cousin that her aunt, the woman who raised her, is missing.

She's already lost her parents tragically in a house fire when we were twelve. Now this. How much trauma can one person endure in a lifetime?

Maggie has been traveling abroad for a few days, and even though we have kept in touch via text messages and phone calls, I've kept her in the dark. The last thing I want to do is mess up her trip and fill her with unnecessary worry. I intended to tell her earlier, but her flight got delayed. Of course.

But it's been three days. She deserves to know.

I answer.

The screen blinks twice before Maggie's face appears, slightly pixelated. She's framed by the hotel room's sheer white curtains fluttering behind her.

"Buongiorno!" she sing-songs, grinning. I haven't smiled in three days, but seeing her excitement … my lips tick upwards on their own. "Okay, that sounded cheesy." She laughs at herself, which she has always been very good at. "Don't hate me, but I've already had gelato twice today. Once at the airport and then on the way to the hotel. I'm addicted."

I roll my eyes. "Sounds so amazing. I'm sorry you got in later than you wanted. What time is it over there?"

Maggie glances at her watch, and props the phone up on something. "It's almost eleven-thirty. It's okay. I'm sure the jetlag will catch up with me eventually, but I think I'm going to go out until it does. Why not? As they say, when in Rome. Or Florence," she answers through a small laugh as she sits at a table, her big blue eyes and blonde hair adding to her allure. The woman was born with it.

Maggie Colbert is every man's dream girl. She's Barbie tall mixed with Christie Brinkley from the eighties. Her megawatt smile and bubbly personality puts anyone around her at ease. A stark contrast to my short and curvy frame, chubby chipmunk cheeks, and sassy attitude. Unruly dark brown curls that I got from my dad and boring brown eyes only add to the yin and yang of who we are.

We couldn't be more different if we tried. But the love we have for each other is unmatched.

"That sounds like fun," I reply, trying my best to sound excited.

But she's known me for far too long and notices my mood.

"Rose, what's going on?" she asks as she lifts the phone, carrying it with her.

I watch her through the screen, unpacking and getting ready for the adventure of a lifetime throughout Europe. A trip my mom gifted us. Her adventures started in France, and now she's in Florence. We had the entire trip planned, but my deadline changed with my most recent book. So, being the brave, independent woman that she is, she went alone.

I've always admired her strength. How she not only survived but thrived after losing both of her parents twenty years ago. She is incredibly inspiring. To me and everyone she meets.

She's my best friend, my family, and the one person who can read me like a book.

Repositioning myself, I roll onto my side and rest my phone against the lamp on my bedside table. I tuck my hand under the pillow. "How do you know me so well?"

"Well, when you're raised together and start your periods on the same day, you're linked for life." She gives me a sad smile.

The tears well up instantly. She notices and sits down on the bed. "Ah, Rose. What's going on? Why are you crying?"

My fingertips brush against my cheeks as I wipe away the tears. "Mom's missing." It's the first time I've uttered the words out loud.

And somehow, that makes it very real.

A sob lodges as a vast emptiness opens up in me.

Her eyes explode in shock. "Wait, what?" She adjusts herself on the bed, shifting as the high spirits she had minutes ago vanish. "What do you mean, missing?"

Juno immediately notices the tears and sleepily moves to get closer, snuggling up against my body. I tuck him into my stomach, rubbing his back. "Remember, she went to that conference at the Black Onyx?"

"Yeah," she confirms as her eyes soften with concern, watching me.

"Well, they had a formal event to finish the conference, and that was the last time anyone saw her. I reported her missing when she didn't show up for brunch the next day."

"That's really unlike her." Maggie hinges forward, resting her chin in her hand. Sharing this with her is oddly comforting, and the loneliness lessens.

"Which is what alarmed me. I waited at the restaurant for about an hour and tried calling her, but it went straight to voicemail. You know how she is, Maggie. If she's running behind, she always texts, and hates to be late." She chuckles, knowing this about my mom. Maggie has been on the tail end of my mom's wrath when she's been late way too many times to count.

"Anyway, when I got to her house, it was all closed up. I let myself in, and something felt off. I could tell she hadn't been home yet. So, I called the police. Now I'm waiting for a call from the lead detective, Richard Dennison. I'm sure he hates me since I've called every day demanding updates. He promised to call today, but I'm going to call him and let him see how crazy we Sheridan girls can be. I want answers."

"Hell yeah! Don't let them drag their feet on this." She releases a long breath and then bolts off the bed. "I'm coming home."

Grabbing the phone, I move Juno and sit upright. "Maggie, no! Absolutely not."

She's tossing clothes into her suitcase. "You need my help!" she snaps, then falters, her words uneven. "If anything happened to her…"

She turns from the screen, staring out in silence, her shoulders trembling.

Silence hangs on the other end. "You okay?"

She wipes away a stray tear. "Yeah. This is scary."

"I know. It's a lot." Once again, we sit quietly. Her staring off, me staring at her.

"Maggie," I plead as she returns to her phone, "I don't want you to come home. I mean, I would love to have you here, but Mom was so happy to send you on this trip. She loves you so much and would be disappointed if she knew you didn't stay. And besides, there's nothing to do right now, anyway. Before you called, I was sitting here staring at the ceiling fan." I manage a small, unconvincing laugh, doing my best to bring things back to normal.

"Stop trying to make me feel better."

"I always do." And she's right. Growing up, when Maggie would cry herself to sleep, missing her parents, I would do anything to put a smile on her face. It killed me to see her crying and grieving. Lightening her mood became my life's mission. Sometimes it would work. Sometimes not.

But we didn't marinate in grief. Or sadness when anything bad would happen. We are most definitely a brush-it-off-and-power-through type of family. Which probably isn't healthy. But it's who we are.

So if my mom doesn't return home, I'm not so sure I'll be able to brush it off.

I'm watching her, waiting to see what she'll say. "Okay." She looks at the screen and offers me a restrained smile. "I'll stay. But you'd better keep me updated. As soon as you talk to the detective, call me. I'm serious."

"Yes, ma'am." As she unpacks again, I try to steer the conversation elsewhere. "Show me your room. Do you have a nice view?" I settle back onto the bed.

She throws her head back. "Unfortunately, no. Aunt Diane confirmed that she booked a room with a view of the Arno River, but this is what I got." She moves across the room, holding the phone to her chest, blocking my view. Next thing I see is Maggie pulling back the same thin white curtain she was in front of when she answered. Along with a brick wall through a window. "Charming, huh?"

"Oh no! You need to complain to someone. That is not what Mom booked."

"Nah. It's okay. I'm only here for a few days, then it's off to Rome!" Her change in mood and obvious enthusiasm fill me with happiness for her.

"Please be careful. You mentioned you are going out. Did you meet someone to hang out with? And please say it's not a guy."

"No, it's not a guy." We laugh because we both know that at some point, she will indeed meet a man. "Her name is Katerina, and she's solo traveling also, so it works out. We are meeting in the hotel bar for drinks, and then we'll see where the wind takes us." She pauses briefly. "Have you called and told Niko about your mom?"

"Niko? Why would I call him?" The question comes out sharper than I intended, and I immediately regret it, given the pained expression on Maggie's face. But Niko is a sore subject with me, and Maggie knows this. He was my last serious relationship. We dated for close to a year before he dumped me. I'm pretty positive he was cheating on me, but he wouldn't admit it. His parting words were that he couldn't be with me anymore.

It was so out of left field.

I thought there was a good chance he was the one. I started dating him in the middle of researching and shadowing a cop for my newest book.

A cop with whom I had a definite connection.

A cop who was quite possibly the most handsome man I had ever met.

A cop who almost kissed me.

A cop whom I argued with for the whole three weeks after that almost kiss.

The amount of attraction and chemistry was unreal.

At the time, I was talking to Niko, and I felt something for him. But then, I got assigned to shadow the hot cop, and POOF! I was ready and willing to put Niko in the rearview mirror.

But the cop rejected me. After our 'almost kiss,' we had quite the push and pull. I must have misread the whole initial attraction because he ghosted me after my time was up. I dove right in with Niko.

Only to have my heart broken.

Needless to say, at thirty-two, I have been very unlucky in love.

And Maggie knows all of this. So, the fact that she is asking about Niko is strange.

I groan, mad at myself for being short. "Sorry, Maggie. That came out rude."

A warm smile stretches. "It's okay. You have a lot on your mind. I just thought maybe since you guys dated and since I'm not there, you might go to him for comfort." She shrugs.

"He is the last person I want comfort from."

A small, fleeting smile crosses her lips as she walks into the bathroom, emptying her cosmetics. The mood of the phone call switches, full of an awkward strain. I watch her, and a pain of selfishness settles in my gut.

Maybe I should have agreed to have her come home.

I want someone here with me. But she needs to be in Italy. Exploring the world.

As I'm about to end the call, the screen lights up with the words *Unknown Number.*

It can only mean one thing.

The detective is calling. *It's about time!*

"Hey Maggie, I've gotta go. The detective is finally calling. Which is good. Now I don't have to raise any hell."

She nods and smiles. "You should anyway. Let me know what they say. I'm not meeting Katerina for another thirty minutes. Love you."

"Love you."

And with that, I click the green button.

Chapter Two
5:42 p.m.

Rose

With shaking hands, I bring the phone up to my ear. My fingers are clammy from the nerves coursing through me.

"Hello?" The greeting wobbles as I climb out of bed.

"Hello, Ms. Sheridan. Richard Dennison here."

"I was just getting ready to call you."

"Yes, I'm sure you were." Sarcasm drips from those five words. *He's so sick of me.*

I hold my breath and pace my bedroom, biting my thumbnail. Juno's curious gaze drags back and forth, watching me. I'm trying hard to sound in control, and I'm anything but. My stomach flips-flops, waiting to hear what news, if any, this detective has to share. It could be anything. Possible scenarios race through my mind like a train barreling down tracks.

She's dead.

They know nothing.

They found her!

And she's alive!

They have a possible lead.

Maybe they discovered some sort of clue.

"Ms. Sheridan. Are you there?"

Crap, he was talking, and I totally zoned out. "Yep. Still here. Could you repeat that? I'm so sorry. I guess I'm just a little stressed. And for good reason. I've been waiting for you guys to call me." A smear of red catches my attention. A cuticle, split and bleeding. Perfect. Another casualty of anxiety. With a sharp exhale, I head into the adjoining bathroom in search of a Band-Aid.

"Understandable." His voice on the other end is low and steady, worn around the edges like someone who's seen too much in life. In his line of work, that isn't surprising. There's a roughness there like maybe from years of smoking. Yet underneath it, there's a gentleness. Something about it makes me breathe easier.

He continues. "I apologize. Just know that we are working around the clock on this."

Yeah, okay.

I gotta admit; he has always sounded sincere, which is helping my anger.

Adhering the bandage to my thumb, my impatience wins out, and I blurt out the one question I want the answer to most of all. "Did you find her?" I climb back into my bed, back against the headboard, and grab Juno for support and comfort. I swallow hard and brace myself, anticipating whatever news he has.

He exhales, then pauses. "No, Ms. Sheridan. I really wish I were calling to tell you that. However …" He trails off. "I understand it's late afternoon, but we found something in the parking garage—well, a few somethings—and we need you to identify them. Are you able to come down to the precinct?"

My breath catches, with no means of escape. As I sit dumbfounded, he continues. "Cal Masters will be here as well. We are working on the case together. If I recall, you shadowed him a year ago?"

His name throws me into a coughing fit.

The cop.

The one I just got done thinking about while on the phone with Maggie. If I'm being honest, I think about Cal ... a lot. But right now, I have to throw these thoughts straight out the window because my mom deserves all my attention.

I clear my throat. "Yes, I did."

"I figured you might be more comfortable with him there. Since you are familiar with each other."

I scoff. *Familiar with each other?* Sure. If familiar means we kissed, and he stopped it, sending me drowning in my humiliation ... then yeah, sure. I guess we are familiar with each other.

The truth of the matter is, I was in the thick of writing my current thriller novel, *Fear Will Become You*, and I had to research the day in the life of a cop. I contacted the precinct, and they agreed as long as I signed a contract and an NDA.

I happily did both.

The first time I saw Cal, the world just ... stopped. He's thirty-seven, tall, broad-shouldered, and built in a quiet, effortless way that doesn't need to prove itself. His smooth, light-brown skin caught the light like polished bronze. And then there are his eyes. God, those green eyes nearly knocked me backward. If Jackson Avery had the body of Thor ... that was Cal.

You see where I'm coming from?

We got along wonderfully for the first few days. Sparks were flying all over the place. When he looked at me ... immediate somersault in my gut. I had never felt that before. For anyone. Not even Niko.

Then, after his shift one night, we went to get a drink. There was flirting, light touches, hair flipping, and a hand on my knee. All the signals that he was interested were there. God knows, I threw out my own. But then outside the bar, we lingered, his hand squeezed my waist, we leaned in, our mutual breath danced, and I thought, 'This is it!'

He pulled away.

After that, he apologized, got back on his bike, and left me on the curb, embarrassed and confused. The next day, his entire personality changed. We went from friendly and flirty to enemies in the blink of an eye. It was total emotional whiplash.

It ended up being the longest month of my life. Being around him, gawking at him, smelling him (because, God, he smelled divine), was torture. And knowing that I wanted more, and he didn't, obviously irritated the crap out of me and caused my sarcastic combativeness to come out. So we were at each other's throats. I could tell my being there bothered him. And he let me know it.

Which is going to make what I say next sound completely insane. But I don't care. It needs to happen.

"Actually," I start, squaring my shoulders, "I have an idea."

There's a pause on the other end and his sigh practically hums through the phone. "All right. Let's hear it."

"If I recall correctly, my contract hasn't expired yet."

He exhales again, the sound laced with suspicion. "I believe you still have a few weeks left, yes."

"Perfect." I sit up straighter, adrenaline kicking in. "Then, I want to be there in person to help. I know my mom better than anyone else. I could be a real asset to the investigation."

"Ms. Sheridan, I don't think—"

"This isn't up for debate," I cut in. "You can use the same excuse as before. I'm shadowing for my book. It's a perfect cover."

I chew on my thumbnail, waiting for him to respond, my pulse thudding in my ears. The idea hit me like lightning during an unavoidable call with my publisher earlier today (that I got nothing out of), and it's been burning a hole in my chest ever since. Sitting at home, pacing, harassing the station for updates—none of that is helping.

I need to do something.

I need to be there.

And if that means working side by side with Cal again, so be it. I'll deal with him. For my mom.

I reach down to scratch behind Juno's ears. "So," I say, forcing brightness into my voice, "when do you want me there?"

He hesitates, then chuckles in defeat. "You're not going to take no for an answer, are you?"

"No, sir. I'm really not."

"Well then," he says, resigned, "the sooner the better. How about one hour?"

I glance down at my clothes—jeans, a one-shouldered sweater, hair barely brushed. The bare minimum. But at least I'm not in pajamas. "One hour works."

"Good. We'll see you soon, Ms. Sheridan." The line clicks dead.

Juno tilts his little head, brown eyes blinking up at me full of nothing but loyalty and love.

"How is this happening, little man?" I whisper.

He just stares, unbothered as usual.

I scoop him into my arms, swing my legs off the bed, and take a deep breath. My entire body feels tight, coiled like a spring ready to snap.

Two reasons.

All the unanswered questions about my mom.

And the one man I'm not sure I'm ready to face again.

Chapter Three
One Year Earlier

Rose

Nerves swarm all through my body as I wait outside the bar. Cal texted me a few minutes ago, warning me he might be late. He's stuck on the case he's working on.

Balancing my weight on my left heel, I rock back and forth, chewing on my nail. While riding in his cruiser back to the station, I about died when he asked me out for a drink. Turns out I wasn't imagining all the flirting, light touches, and other stuff he'd been doing.

Because this man.

God, this man.

This attraction is surreal. And I get it. I'm a thirty-one-year-old woman with a host of bad boyfriends in my rear-view mirror.

Not one of them has left me reeling when I'm not with them.

Not one of them has looked at me the way Cal does.

Not one of them has made me feel … so alive.

A small smile crosses my lips, full of anticipation, as the low growl of an engine makes my pulse skip. A man pulls to the curb atop a sleek black Honda sport motorcycle that gleams under the streetlights. Those same lights reflecting off his polished helmet. He kills the engine and swings his leg over, pulling off his helmet, revealing his beautiful face.

My mouth goes completely dry.

He smirks while taking off his gloves, shoving them into his helmet, as his gaze drifts down and then back up my body.

I bite my lip because … dear Lord, he looks good. The black leather jacket, the entrance, the quiet confidence—as if he's walked straight out of a movie. I can't stop myself from smiling.

"Nice ride," I say, trying not to sound too impressed. Although I am very, very impressed.

His lip twitches. "Gets me from A to B."

With a cool, casual swagger, he approaches me and stands close. Almost too close. We stare, and an electric current pulses through me, like lightning. He's glaring at me in a way he hasn't since the day we met.

He's so stupidly tall that I have to crane my neck to meet his eyes. "I didn't know you rode a bike."

"You didn't ask," he replies with that deep rasp that I've come to crave. What I love about Cal is that he is one of those people who's cool and doesn't know it. You know what I mean, right? There's nothing fake or pretentious about him. The man just wakes up in the morning and waltzes through life exuding confidence without trying. Other than his looks, it's the most attractive thing about him.

Yes, I've made a list. Don't judge.

"Where did you park? Not too far, I hope," he inquires while looking around the busy street. Cars line either side of the road with Cal taking the last spot available in front of the restaurant.

I point in the direction of my car. "Just right there. Only four spots away."

"Okay, good." He jerks his head toward the bar. "You ready?"

Well, that's a loaded question. Am I ready? Yes, Cal. I. Am. Ready.

I nod, and his hand lands on the small of my back, leading me inside. His palm flattens, and heat spreads everywhere, making my thoughts swim.

We stroll inside the little bar, and low lights mixed with soft music encase every nook and cranny. The corners have secluded booths, and other patrons occupy the many bar stools. In another corner, a small stage rests, ready for the next band scheduled to play. The whole bar is dark, sultry, seductive and makes you feel sexy as soon as you walk in.

It screams passion without trying.

It's private without being secretive.

It's easy without trying too hard.

Just like Cal.

The pent-up energy I've carried since the day I met him finally eases, and I let myself breathe. Being with him these last few days has been torture. Each morning, seeing him triggers a rush of attraction that courses through me. But we were working (well, he's working. I'm just taking notes), and I didn't want to let my guard down. But now. Well, I'm free to be myself.

Cal picks a table in the corner of this lush bar, tucked away from the other patrons. I like it. It's private and out of the way. And of course, being the gentleman he is, he pulls my chair out for me. He rounds the table and grabs the small drink menu standing upright. "Order whatever you want. Drinks are on me tonight."

I nod and grin, not about to argue. Let's be serious; I will do anything this man asks. His green eyes pierce into me, and my cheeks heat, which I'm hoping he didn't catch in this low light. "Okay, but I gotta warn you. I like a good-quality bourbon."

"Well, lucky me then. I get to have drinks with a gorgeous woman who has good taste." He shifts in his seat, hunching forward. His hand inches across the table until his knuckles lightly brush against my arm. Goosebumps erupt. "You look incredibly beautiful tonight," he rasps.

Oh, Lord. My stomach flips at his words. Bravery fills my soul as I dance my fingertips along the top of his hand. One of his eyebrows raises, his intense stare locking with mine. "Thank you," I whisper out as gratitude fills me. It's the only reply I can come up with, but it means so much. Because no man has ever looked at me with such reverence and told me I was 'incredibly beautiful.'

Not one.

As the night wears on, we talk. About everything and nothing. He makes me laugh—really laugh—and it's so foreign. And I do the same for him. Not once in my adult life have I thought I was funny. Until tonight.

It's been so long since I felt this kind of connection and ease with someone on a date. For a couple of hours, I can almost believe we're just two people out for a drink, not drowning in work and adult responsibilities.

The waiter makes his way back over to us, pointing to our empty glasses. "Another one?"

"Water for me, thanks," Cal replies, covering his glass with his hand. "But you go ahead."

Typically, one glass of bourbon on a date is my norm, but this date is different. It's like I can let the real Rose shine through. When Maggie and I go out, three small glasses of bourbon are my norm. But not with anyone else. Especially a man. Plus, I don't think we are leaving anytime soon, which will give the alcohol time to leave my system before I drive.

Tonight with Cal, I'm relaxed. And free.

"Um, sure. I'll have another." The waiter nods and scurries away, leaving us alone once again.

Resting my chin on my palm, I take him in. And trust me, there is a lot of him. And I want it all.

The alcohol coursing through me gives me courage. "Soooo, Cal Masters..."

He matches my body language, inching closer. His hand finds my thigh under the table, and squeezes. The air stalls in my lungs. "Yes, Rose Sheridan," he replies.

"Are you going to kiss me tonight?"

I shock myself. *Where did that come from? Who am I?*

His lips curl into a grin that borders on evil. "Only if the lady grants me permission."

Permission granted.

I shift closer to him. "She would," I purr.

His hand travels up my thigh as we both tilt our chins. His lips part and—

"Here ya go!" We jolt backward as the waiter, with impeccable timing, sets down my drink. "Is there anything else I can get you two this evening?"

"We are good. Thank you," Cal replies. The hint of annoyance is undeniable.

Actually, the interruption was a gift because I need to put the brakes on how fast this night is going. And it's not that I have no desire to kiss Cal. Because, God, I do. I really, really do. But I want to get to know him a little better first.

Cal's hand stays on my leg, as his thumb rubs in small circles.

I grasp my drink, studying him across the table. The way his broad shoulders slump a little now that he's relaxed, how his expression softens when he forgets to guard them. He's different in this setting. So unlike the work version of Cal that I have been getting day in and day out.

I like this Cal. Very much.

Tapping his finger, he gives me a quizzical look. "So, what have you learned about being a detective in the past week?"

I snicker. "Well, it's only been a few days, but you guys deal with a lot of domestic violence." He shrugs in agreement. "And there is a lot of sitting in your car. Just waiting. More than I expected."

He grins. "No lies there."

"And I was really hoping there would be more donut shop breaks."

He laughs. A full-on belly laugh. *See … I'm funny.*

"I always wondered where that stereotype came from." He slowly regains his composure. "But seriously, do you think any of what you've seen you can use in your book?"

I nod while sipping my bourbon. "Yes, absolutely."

His fingers graze mine across the table. "I can't wait to read it."

I tilt my head. "You read?" Because if this hunk of a man reads, let's just get this over with. Yes, I will marry you, Cal.

"Only Rose Sheridan books."

Oomph, I'm in trouble.

"So," I say, drifting forward once again, "earlier, I told you way too much about my love life. That it's messy, complicated, and nonexistent. What about you?"

His brow arches. "My love life?"

"Yes," I press. "Don't tell me you've been too busy playing detective your whole life. You've dated, right?"

Faintly he smirks, but his face is blank. "Once or twice."

"That's vague." I grin, still holding my bourbon, swirling the brown liquid around. "Spill."

He exhales, staring at his glass for far too long. Then, his hand leaves my thigh, and he settles back in his chair. Disappointment surges through me. "They don't last. The job gets in the way. And"—he glares off into the void of the crowded bar—"when people find out how dangerous it can get, they don't usually stick around."

Something about his tone and change in body language is throwing me off. It's quiet and raw, and it tugs at me. "So what, you just gave up?"

Ugh, why did I bring this up? It's like he's constructed a sudden wall in a matter of seconds.

Don't give up on me, Cal. I'm here. I'm not leaving.

"Not exactly." His stare lifts, steady, locking with mine. "I stopped pretending I could have both. The work and the someone. But maybe…"

He stops his thought, taking a swig of his water. I press some more. "You sound like you don't think you deserve it."

He doesn't answer. But his silence speaks volumes.

I want to reach across the table, touch his hand and tell him he's wrong. Instead, I take the path of least resistance and sip my drink, swallowing the words with the burn of liquor.

After some more tense conversation, Cal suggests ending the evening. He gulps down the rest of his water. "I hate to do this, but I have an early morning meeting tomorrow."

Well, okay then. I guess that's his way of saying, 'We're done here.'

"Ummm … sure." With major disappointment coursing through me, I reach around to grab my purse. All the chemistry and desire of the evening seems like it was weeks in the past and not minutes ago. Even the once sensual atmosphere of the bar now feels suffocating.

We both stand at the same time. "I'll walk you out," he offers, not meeting my face.

Touchy-feely Cal has vanished because he guides me out of the bar and into the noisy street without laying a finger on me. Instantly, something has shifted. The flirty, tender, teasing version of Cal I'd been wrapped up in moments ago is gone.

Maybe it was the mention of his dating life. Dragging that up—like the absolute idiot I am—hit a nerve I didn't know was there. It might've stirred up something painful, or maybe he's wrestling with his own history, things he's not ready to share.

I don't know. But I wish I did.

All I know is the mood is different now. Distant. Like we've slipped backward a few steps without meaning to. And now I'm terrified of losing whatever fragile thing we've started to build.

THE STORM WE BREATHE 25

We linger on the sidewalk outside, neither of us talking. The night air is cool, the street buzzing faintly with passing cars. His bike is right in front of us, so I wonder if he's going to bolt without so much as a hug.

Which will really twist me in knots.

I pull my keys out of my purse. "My car is parked right down there," I tell him, even though we had this discussion earlier, but I'm at a loss for words with his weird vibe. He offers me a tight grin and gestures for me to walk on.

Side by side, we trudge down the bustling street. He shoves his hand into his pocket as the other clutches his helmet. A quick glance his way, and I can see the conflict simmering beneath.

We stride in awkward silence until we get to my car, which feels like an eternity, even though it was only half a block away. I hit the unlock button on my key fob, swallowing down the unease. The car chirps.

This isn't ending the way I thought it would, but I have to at least say goodbye and thank him for the evening.

As I reach for the car door, he moves in. His shadow slips over me, swallowing the space that separated us. He's so close, and the heat rolling off him curls around me, slow and intoxicating.

My breath stutters. Words vanish. "Um ... th-thank you for—"

Without warning, he catches my wrist and spins me. Our bodies collide, chest to chest, and the impact sends an electric spark racing straight through my body.

We lock eyes.

We stare.

We breathe.

The war raging inside him is something I can't unsee. He's so torn and lost.

His fingertips trace up my arm. Goosebumps erupt with his slow touch. Gorgeous green eyes pierce through me, then they skim to my lips and back again. My pulse stutters as his other arm hooks around my waist, tugging me to him.

He moves closer, inch my inch.

The world narrows, and I forget to breathe.

This is it.

Finally.

My eyes shut, waiting. Hot breath skates over my face as his lips brush over mine. Featherlight and brief.

I wait.

And wait.

And wait.

He pulls back.

I blink as his jaw tightens. "We shouldn't," he mumbles as he swallows, squeezing his eyes. "This isn't professional."

What the heck?

The words land like a physical blow. I force a nod, pretending this isn't shattering me. When I step back, his arms fall limp at his side, taking his warmth with him. Then the anger flares. I huff out a laugh. "You're joking?"

He hesitates, rubbing the back of his neck, and I know he wants to say more. I mean, my God, an explanation would be nice. But he only stares as his jaw tightens. Then he winces and shakes his head. "Goodnight, Rose."

"Wait, what? You're leaving?" I spit out, the rejection morphing into annoyance. And in a split second, he's gone. I watch him retreat, walking to his bike. Head down, shoulders slumped, hand in his pocket. "Cal!" I cry out. He doesn't look back. His bike roars to life as he zooms away in the darkness, his taillights disappearing, leaving me with a ton of questions.

I stand there numb, angry, and dejected. *Did I do something wrong? Why? Why did he change his mind so quickly?*

This is going to drive me bonkers because now I'm rehashing and doubting what I said, how I acted, all of it. Plus, I'm angry. How dare he toy with my emotions like that!

My feet won't move, cemented to the concrete as I process the last few minutes. Every part of me hums with a mix of wanting him and needing him. Desire and outrage blur together until I don't know where one ends and the other begins.

That's when a voice cuts through.

"Rose?"

The sound of my name being called through the heartbreak forces me to whip around. And shock of all shocks … Niko is here. He looks at me the way someone does when they care too much but won't say it out loud. "You okay?" he asks, his tone sweet.

Niko and I had been talking for a while. He's sweet, charming, and the kind of guy you could almost picture a future with. Almost.

But then Cal showed up, and suddenly it was … Niko who?

Now he's here.

And Cal's … not.

I swallow hard, blinking back the sting. "Yeah. I'm tired. That's all."

He steps closer cautiously, his presence feeling secure where Cal's absence left me unsteady. "I don't believe you," he says with a knowing smirk on his face. *How did he know I was lying?* "Tell me, what happened?"

With a dismissive motion, I wave my hand. "Oh nothing. You know … rejection." I shrug. "It can sting."

Another step and, with a tentative reach, he swipes the stray tear tracking down my cheek that I didn't even realize was there. Then he smiles. His big blue eyes are searching, full of concern and longing. They are beautiful, and I could get lost in them.

It's small, but my heart cracks open. Just a little.

"You don't have to be alone tonight." His words are soothing, husky, circling me like a blanket. "Come out with me. The evening doesn't have to end. What do you say?"

And with the way he's looking at me right now, I know he could. Plus, I can't drive yet.

I glance down the street where Cal disappeared. It's empty. All hope I had for us twists, and is now torn and heavy.

I turn back to Niko, at the kindness he's showing. This isn't how I envisioned my night going.

But Cal left.

"Yes," I whisper.

Chapter Four

6:28 p.m.

Rose

"You be a good boy while I'm gone." Juno stares up at me with the most pathetic look on his face while I rub his ears. As soon as I grabbed my purse, he knew I was leaving. Then the puppy-dog eyes started.

I give him a sad smile before I touch up my red lipstick, grab my keys and purse, and head out the door.

I'm a complete wreck. My hands won't stop shaking as I approach my car. I try to convince myself to stay calm, to keep breathing, but my thoughts won't listen. Images of Mom flash in my mind. Her laugh, her perfume, the way she'd hum when she was cooking. Each memory feels like a knife twisting deeper.

As I sink into the driver's seat, my phone chimes. I swipe the screen, expecting a text, but it's a weather alert instead.

Severe storms approaching. Take shelter immediately.

My stomach dips. I hate storms. The forecast is calling for one of the worst systems to hit this part of Ohio in decades. Torrential rain, dangerous winds, the works. And it's supposed to last for hours.

Well, the weather will match my mood, so there's that.

With my thoughts a chaotic jumble, I drive to the precinct. A clap of thunder off in the distance catches my attention. Approaching the red light, I peer out the windshield; the sky fills my vision. The distant, dark clouds look threatening. I have to get there sooner rather than later.

As I wait at a red light, my phone chimes again. This time, it's a text. From Niko.

Seriously? I don't need anymore anxiety today. And communicating with my ex will without a doubt give me anxiety.

> Niko: Hey. I heard about your mom. You okay?

"Really?" I toss my phone onto the console, not ready to reply yet. And it's not that I don't still have some lingering feelings for him. I do.

I probably always will. Everything that went down is weird because I didn't get any closure. And when that happens, the leftover emotions scab over, leaving visible scars.

But I know that scar has to fade in order to move on.

I mean, it's sweet that he's asking about my mom. I'm sure he saw it on the news. I guess replying wouldn't be that big of a deal. Right?

Okay, fine! The light's still red, so I shoot out my reply.

> Me: Hi. Yes, it's been scary. I'm so worried about my mom. Thank you for reaching out. On my way to meet with the head detective now. Hopefully, he has some answers.

HONK!

Startled, I peek at the stoplight, and it's green. I wave a signal of apology to the car behind me as I roll forward, tossing my phone. His reply chimes in, but now I'm pulling into the parking lot and my stomach immediately starts churning.

I read his text.

> Niko: If you need anything, let me know. I miss you, Rose.

My eye roll is so big it probably made a noise. *He misses me? Seriously?* Why is he saying this to me now? What does he expect me to say? 'I miss you too'? Because, in all honesty, I do miss him.

But I'm not sure if I miss *him* or everything that comes with being in a relationship. The closeness, the intimacy. Having someone else in your corner. No matter the cost to them.

Yep, that's it. Not the cheater.

Shaking the thoughts away, I retrieve my purse from the passenger seat. I'm not doing this with him again. And like Rachel's mom said on *Friends,* 'Once a cheater, always a cheater.'

With the decision made, I grab my phone and throw it into my crossbody, ignoring his text. I'll reply later. Pulling down the visor, I double-check my lipstick one last time.

Vomit sits at the base of my stomach as I grip the door handle and stare ahead at the entrance.

Information about my mom is inside that building.

"As I live and breathe. If it isn't Rose Sheridan, here. In my precinct. Again."

Upon hearing my name on his tongue, all raspy and deep like I remember, I jolt out of the chair.

Cal is leaning against the doorway, arms linked over his chest, ankles crossed, dressed in all black like he always is.

That used to annoy me. People who only wear black all the time. But Cal, wearing nothing but black, turns my insides out. And here he is one year later, black shirt, black tie, black jeans, and black boots. Promising to be the dark knight I know he is. The only color on him is the brown leather shoulder holster strapped to his muscles.

Plus, he is staring at me like he wants to kill me. I'm sure he hates me. *Well, the feeling is mutual, sir.*

I square my shoulders, ready for the standoff. "Cal," is all the greeting I'm willing to offer him. "You remembered me. I'm flattered, truly," I say mockingly as I raise my hand to my chest. My heart may have skipped a beat when I saw him, but his eyes narrowed into slits and his nostrils flared. Full of what, I don't know. Anger? It's like we've snapped right back to where we left off a year ago.

Fantastic.

He looks away and drags a hand over the not-quite-five-o'clock shadow on his jaw. During our time together, I couldn't read this man. Hot one minute. Ice-cold the next. Apparently, he's still a walking mystery novel with no final chapter.

He pushes off the doorframe and starts down the hallway without looking back, and—lucky me—I trail after him.

A low chuckle slips out of him. "Did you really think I'd forget? You were the bane of my existence for a month when you shadowed us for your book."

"Bane of your existence? Little dramatic, don't you think?" And no mention of the best date I ever had that ended … badly. He rounds a corner, which opens up into another hallway. I continue to follow him through the maze, the hustle and bustle of a police station charges along around us.

He ignores my question. "Why are you following me?"

"Dennison didn't tell you?"

"It's Denny."

"Denny?" Now I'm confused. "Who's Denny?"

"You know Richard Dennison. Or Denny. It's his nickname around here."

I roll my eyes. *Okay, fine, whatever the man's name is.* His long tree-trunk legs are propelling him forward, and I'm practically running to keep up with him. "You're assigned to my mother's case."

He abruptly stops, and I collide with a wall of muscle that feels like steel. He spins on his heels to face me, and I stumble back a step. But it's his face that's the same as it was one year ago. Still rugged, chiseled, and with a jaw that could cut glass. "Yes, I know. Diane Sheridan."

At the sound of my mom's name, I freeze. Hearing it said out loud, for whatever reason, means she still exists. Hopefully, alive. My lips press together and tremble slightly.

He notices.

That hard exterior shell cracks slightly, and the toughness in his face eases. "I'm sorry you're going through this."

I nod, then look down at my feet, since seeing his concern is messing with my head. My emotions are all over the place right now. "Thank you," I drag in a long, stabilizing breath, still refusing to meet his eyes. "Anyway, Dennison … Sorry, Denny, is allowing me to shadow you while you are working the case. Well, actually, correction, I demanded it."

"Of course you did," he barks out, then swivels and treks down the hall. I'm hot on his trail.

"I promise to stay out of your way."

"Unlikely."

"You won't hear a peep out of me."

"Heard that once before."

We're standing at the threshold of his office as he shifts to face me. But not before he briefly roams down my body and back up.

Seriously, if I'd blinked, I would have missed it. But I didn't. "Go ask him yourself. He called me an hour ago and asked me to come down because they found something that they think might be Mom's." Those last few words come out strained, barely audible, as I squint away.

When I get the nerve to look back up at him, his eyes have grown tender, and he's inched closer, and my pulse trips over itself.

I can't let my guard down, though. Especially with him. "I assumed you knew about all of this. That's how Denny made it sound when he called me."

He grunts as his face becomes stone again. "Denny isn't here. He got pulled away for an emergency meeting involving a different case, but will be back. Stay here. I'm going to call him and straighten this out. And by that I mean, a snowball's chance in hell this is going to happen." He marches backward and slams the door in my face. Literally in my face. The wood hit my nose.

I rub it. "Ouch." Well, that felt like the Cal I knew. And what was that almost affectionate look he gave me?

I sit on one of the chairs lined up against the wall. Rubbing my sweaty palms down my jeans, I glance at the door. *Should I listen? I shouldn't. Right?*

Yes, it's wrong. Not cool.

My eyes drift to the ceiling as my knee does a nervous dance.

Ugh!

"Forget it. I have to know." I leap up and press my ear against the cheap wood.

Cal isn't happy as his deep voice carries through the door. Muffled but angry.

"There is no way, Denny. Her being here around me made my life hell when she shadowed us. You know what that did to me. You remember, right?"

What did I do? I mean, yeah, we argued like cats and dogs after the almost kiss, but I didn't think it was that bad.

A 'mm-hmm' follows a few 'uh-huhs.' Then … "Denny, I can't. Please, why does she have to shadow me for this? Why?" Another stretch of silence. "Of course she was being pushy."

Pushy?! Excuse me! I need to find my mom. And why do I have to shadow? *Ummm … because she's my mom, you idiot.* And is spending time with me that bad?

"Fine. But you owe me. It took me months to get over—" A long pause. "I know. I know. I tried. Things are going well. But now—"

Okay, now I'm confused. *What did he have to get over? And he tried what, exactly?*

He sighs. "I won't guarantee this isn't going to end in disaster, but if you think it's a good idea, I'll do it." He sounds so defeated.

Well, geez, Cal. Sorry that my mom's disappearance is an inconvenience to you.

Admittedly, inside, I am screaming with delight because I remember how good a detective he was. My mom's case is in the right hands.

"See you in a minute."

I lean in, pressing my ear to the door, waiting for more. Nothing. Not a sound.

The door flies open. I lose my footing and collide straight into a wall of muscle. Strong arms wrap around me, steadying me like I'm some clumsy extra in a rom-com. "Whoa," he says, practically lifting me off my feet before setting me upright again. His hands linger at my waist, and for one second, I forget how to breathe.

When I finally find my voice, I look up—and yep, there it is. That look. Attraction, curiosity, maybe even that spark I remember from a year ago. But then, as if realizing it, he clenches his jaw, releases me, and steps back like I just announced I have the plague.

"Are you in the habit of eavesdropping, Sheridan?" He sweeps his arm over the threshold, inviting me in.

"I wasn't listening," I lie.

"Mm-hmm."

Sheridan.

That's what he always called me last year. Never Rose. Just my last name.

Sheridan.

I loved it then. *Do I now though?*

Maybe. I don't know.

My attention immediately starts roving over his workspace. I mean, offices are kind of extensions of our own personal lives, right? He spends a lot of time in this tiny room day in and day out. Maybe I can get a glimpse into this man as I wait.

"Why haven't I been in here before?" I ask, thinking back to a year ago and the time we spent together. At the end of the day, I would get in my car and leave. If I ever went inside the station, it was to pee before I would head home. We argued so much that I wanted to get away from him as quickly as possible.

"There was never a reason." *He's right.*

His fingers drum against his thigh as I continue to roam. I have to do something to occupy the negative thoughts in my head about my mom.

Immediately, my eyes land on a picture of him with President Obama that hangs on the wall.

Impressive.

A small red neon sign hangs above the door frame.

Random.

A mug that says World's Best Son.

Sweet.

It's all here. A couple of plants on a filing cabinet, his desk, a swivel chair, piles of paperwork. It's all so methodical, organized, and polished.

Kinda like the man himself.

The moment stretches like taffy as he continues to watch me. It's painfully quiet. I force a polite smile, hoping to diffuse the weird tension. He offers one back, quick and tight. It's as if we both forgot how to act like normal people.

My gaze wanders and lands on a photo sitting near his desk. I can't see it clearly from here, just the edge of a frame and a flash of movement frozen in time. But something about it tugs at me.

Cal's reaction is instant. He follows my gaze, stiffens, then launches across the room. "That's—uh—personal," he mutters, scooping the frame up so fast it blurs.

He opens a drawer, tosses the photo inside, and slams it shut.

My brows rise. "Wow. Not suspicious at all."

For a heartbeat, he doesn't say anything. His back stays to me, shoulders squared, tension rolling off him. Then, quietly, he says, "It's just a photo of me and someone."

I should leave it alone. Right?

Curiosity wins. "Someone important?"

He exhales through his nose, still not facing me. "Someone who mattered once."

Oh.

I open my mouth, then close it again, because what do you even say to that? It's none of my business, anyway.

He clears his throat, avoiding eye contact, and sits at his desk. "Can you please sit down?"

"Sure." I sit.

Slumping back in his chair, he grabs his phone, and rests his ankle on his opposite knee while I try to find something to look at. Or think about.

Another unpleasant silence stretches on for far longer than I am comfortable with, and a nasty habit of mine roars to life as I wait. His voice cuts through my thoughts. "You're picking your nails." My eyes shoot up, and he's staring at me, brow furrowed.

I drop my hands, embarrassed, so of course I start to ... "Now you're biting your lip."

"Boy, you really like to point out all my quirks, don't you?" He only stares. I sigh. "I'm sorry, I'm just very—"

"Nervous," he answers for me. "I remember."

Wait. What? He remembers. Why?

The same look of concern crosses his features. "It's going to be okay, Sheridan. I promise I will do everything to find your mom."

A tightness chokes me as I fight back the tears because now he's brought her up. I plead, "Do you know anything? Any information at all?"

His face falls as he drops his phone on the desk and rests on his forearms. The motion reminds me of the night at the bar. "We should probably wait until Denny gets here."

I nod with emptiness. "It's the not knowing that's the hardest," I confess, then begin to ramble. "Like, is she hurt? Bleeding? Where is she? Or maybe she's d..." I turn away, not saying the word. "I just want answers. Which is why I need to be a part of this. I won't stop until she's found."

He gives me a sad smile. "Me neither. And this can't be easy. On any level."

"No, it's the worst feeling in the world."

He pauses. "Hopeless."

My head snaps to his. He gets it. "Yes. Hopeless."

His whole expression relaxes, touched with something gentler. "Look, before Denny gets here, I wanted you to know that I'm sorry for how I—"

Whatever he was going to apologize for hangs suspended, unfinished, as Denny bursts into the room, panting heavily. As if he'd run all the way here from wherever he was.

"Oh good, you're still here," he heaves out as he holds the doorknob. *Where did he think I would go exactly?*

Denny isn't a tall man. He's of average height but definitely not of average build. You can tell he possesses the type of brute strength that you can just … see. Kinda like he grew up on a farm. Broad shoulders, thick arms and fingers, a wide neck. He's someone I would want on my side if I were in a dark alley. Hands down.

But also, his face carries years of experience. His dark blond hair is thinning, and his deep-set brown eyes have a few extra creases around the edges. But you can tell there is a kindness lurking underneath. He's a handsome older man.

Honestly, he's the type of guy my mom would be interested in.

The sudden thought of my mom maybe never finding love again makes my stomach churn. "I'm still here. No plans of leaving," I answer with determination.

He gives me a tight smile, then turns his attention to Cal. "Let's go down to interrogation room two. I think it's open."

My neck snaps back. "Interrogation room?" I question, concern rattling every syllable. I don't like the sound of that. Talk about in-timidating. I do not want to go into a room where they brow-beat confessions out of criminals. Is that why I'm here? Oh, God! *Do they think I'm a suspect?* I bite my lip.

Cal's attention immediately falls on me, staring, assessing.

He bolts, chasing Denny into the hall.

I watch the two men talking with rapt attention. And yes, also attempting to listen, but they are too far out of earshot. Actually, Cal is talking; Denny agrees. Finally, Denny disappears down the hall as Cal comes back into his office. "He'll be right back."

Keeping his head down, he doesn't look at me. Only sits studying his phone again. I watch him, questioning, not fully understanding.

Did he notice my reaction? He must have. The way his mouth twitches gives it away.

"Did you tell Denny that we should meet here?" I ask, trying to sound casual and failing miserably.

"Yeah." He doesn't even look up from whatever's so fascinating on his phone. "I wanted you to be comfortable."

"That wasn't necessary," I lie, refusing to act like I needed his help.

"Clearly." His tone drips with sarcasm. "But I did it, anyway."

"I didn't ask for your concern," I bite back, folding my arms.

His jaw flexes, that muscle ticking in a way that used to drive me insane. "So this is how it's going to be then? Being combative with me won't help your mom's case."

I force a fake sweet smile. "Cool. Noted. Non-combative Rose reporting for duty. Shall we try small talk then?"

He finally glances up, one eyebrow raised. "We've never been good at that."

"Well, we'd better start practicing. Finding my mom depends on it."

He nods, but the silence that follows is ... uncomfortable.

"So," I say, desperate, "what have you been up to since I last saw you?"

He smirks, leaning back in his chair. "You're looking at it."

God, that confidence. That infuriating, smug confidence.

I shift in my seat, forcing my attention to the window. "We have some bad storms coming."

"Yeah," he says, clicking his tongue. "That's what I hear."

A long pause stretches, and because I clearly have a death wish, I add, "Still a fan of black, I see."

His grin flickers, slow and wicked. "I hate color."

A laugh bursts out of me before I can stop it—half snort, half sigh. "Explains a lot."

He chuckles, low and quiet, breaking the tension somewhat. But then his body goes rigid, and his eyes narrow. "So how's Niko?"

I freeze at his question. Wait. What? Niko? Why is he asking about Niko? How does he *know* about Niko?

"Niko?" I retort. He shrugs. "Why are you asking me about my ex?"

His expression falls as his brows pinch together and my words sink in.

"Your ex?"

"Yes, my ex. We broke up three weeks ago." The defensiveness hits me hard. "How did you even know we were together to begin with?"

He lowers his focus, adjusting his tie that's already straight. "I'm sorry, Sheridan. I shouldn't have said anything."

But I'm not letting this go. "Cal, why are you asking about—"

The words die on my tongue as Denny bursts through the door, a bulging manila envelope clutched in his hand. "Ms. Sheridan, thank you for your patience," he says, completely unaware of what he's just broken apart.

I glance at Cal, silently screaming at the interruption. His jaw tightens, eyes meeting mine for the briefest second before looking away. As if the moment between us had never existed.

Denny shimmies his stalky body around my seat, sitting in the empty chair next to mine. "No problem," I mutter.

He looks up at Cal and smirks. "I hope Cal was keeping you company."

Cal shoots him a disbelieving glance, which morphs into an 'I'm going to kill you' expression. Denny chuckles under his breath as a silent conversation passes between them.

Suddenly, I feel like a third wheel.

Denny turns his attention back to me. "Ms. Sheridan, we want you to know that we are working tirelessly, around the clock, trying to find your mother. Cal here"—he points to the man in black—"has barely slept."

What? He's barely slept? Helping me?

I steal a look at Cal. He only nods. "Good. I expect nothing less."

Denny continues. "We know your mom was last seen at the hotel three nights ago. Where and how she disappeared is what we are trying to piece together."

I find myself picking my fingers again without realizing it. Cal notices, his eyes zeroing in on my hands. "Initially, nothing turned up."

My shoulders sag in defeat. "However, this morning, we received a call from the front desk, stating that a hotel guest turned in a few things they found in the parking garage. We asked them to inform us if anything showed up. So they did."

Without meaning to, my eyes flick to Cal. His brows knit together, worry etched deep. Then his eyes find mine, and for a moment, I can breathe again.

Denny reaches for the manila envelope. "Ms. Sheridan. Are these your mother's belongings?"

One at a time, Denny begins to pull random items out of the envelope.

Items I recognize immediately.

Her glittery pink clutch is first. I run my fingers over the sequins.

Next follows her compact with her initial embossed on the outside. A gift from my father. He sets it on top of the clutch.

Denny's meaty fingers pulls out a gold tube of lipstick. Her signature color. Charlotte Tilbury's Super Fabulous. He sets it next to the compact.

The whole revelation is happening in slow motion.

Next is her red leather Chanel wallet. He sets it down next to the clutch. "It was emptied out."

I nod at his words as tears begin, and my fingertips graze the soft leather. Before I can react further, Cal leaps from his seat and stands right behind me. *How did he figure out I needed comfort?*

His hand rests on the back of my seat.

I sniff through the emotions coursing through me. "This was all that was in the purse. We suspect that when someone found it, they emptied it out. Her ID as well."

"May I?" I ask, pointing to the clutch.

"Of course," Denny answers.

I grab it, unzip the top, and search inside.

The comforting force behind me shifts. "Are you looking for something?" Cal asks.

I nod. "My dad's wedding ring. My mom wouldn't leave the house without it."

Denny glances up at Cal. "I'm sorry, Ms. Sheridan. This is all that was in there."

It's gone. Sadness overwhelms me.

"I know this is hard, and I'm so sorry, but do these items belong to your mother?" Denny asks.

I sniffle and choke out the answer to his loaded question. "Y-Yes. They do."

Denny's hand reaches into the envelope and pulls out a zip-lock bag with a piece of paper inside.

Cal steps closer.

"One more question." Denny rests the bag in front of me. "Is this your mother's handwriting?"

Chapter Five
7:17 p.m.

Cal

To whomever finds this, please give it to the police.
Rose,
Tell Maggie I'm sorry. I tried.
Live your best life.
I love you.

Rose's angelic voice reads the note, each word coming out on a strangled sob.

She pauses for a moment and then hands the note back to Denny. "Yes. That's my mom's handwriting."

My hand tightens around the chair as a way to control myself since all I want to do is touch her. It's euphoric, being this close to her again. Standing behind her only reminds me of our date.

The day I regret most in my whole life.

Pushing that moment out of the recesses of my thoughts—which isn't easy since I think about it almost daily—I redirect my attention to Denny.

Or Richard Dennison.

Denny is the best captain and cop on this force. The man's work ethic is unmatched, and I admire the hell out of him.

People have accused him of being gruff. Rude, even mean at times. And well, they aren't wrong. I think I'm the only one who has seen the more human side. So, I had to tell him to be gentler in his approach to this case. He is a hurry-and-let's-get-the-case-solved kinda guy.

But I don't want Rose to be rushed or upset. So when I see a lone tear fall down her cheek ... it's doing two things to me. One, find and take out the psycho who has kidnapped her mom, and two, trip over my own two feet to get her a tissue.

Which is exactly what I do. The second she becomes upset, I spin to grab one from the windowsill and almost fall on my face handing it to her. Denny snickers, which annoys me.

Because he knows.

He knows that the last time Rose and I worked together, I fell in love with her.

He knows that I rejected her on that sidewalk.

He knows my insecurities about relationships.

He knows that after our almost-kiss, I was an idiot and pushed her away by being a first-class jerk to her, which only caused us to argue. I'm sure she thinks I hate her, and I wouldn't blame her. I hate myself.

And why?

Because the day before our date, I found out she was talking to someone. Niko. One night, while we were working, she left her phone on the passenger seat of my car while she used the bathroom at a Wendy's. And okay, yes, I looked. It was Niko. There were texts. Lots of them. Texts you send to someone you are interested in and close to dating. I panicked at the thought of missing my chance, so I asked her out as soon as she got back in the car.

But then, that night, as I held her in my arms, and her lips grazed mine, I realized something. Who was I to waltz in and implode her life? Or any plans she may have had. Plus, my luck with women has been awful. Rose is perfect. Too perfect. It felt wrong to pull her into my complicated life and job. So I bolted.

You don't have to say it. Stupid, I know.

Once our month-long stint was up, I bid her farewell and dove headfirst into the dating scene to rid myself of thoughts of her.

Didn't work.

Because no one compares to Rose Sheridan.

Then, one day, about a month later, I decided to shoot my shot and reach out to her. First, to apologize for being a complete idiot. And to ask her out. As long as she didn't hang up on me, which was a real possibility. I was a hot mess that day while her phone rang. My palms were sweating as I watched the snow fall outside my office window. Then someone answered.

"Hello." A man's greeting hit my ear, and it felt like someone punched me in the gut.

"Ummm … hey. Is Rose available?" Hope filled my question as I was praying I had the wrong number. Or maybe this was a family member or something.

"She's in the shower, but this is her boyfriend. Anything I can help you with?"

Instantly, I stiffened as heat shot straight to my brain. I wanted to know if this was exactly who I thought it was. "Is this Niko?"

"Yes." He paused, then asked, irritation lacing his tone, "Do I know you?"

It was at that moment I knew I had screwed up. I blew my one and only chance with the woman of my dreams. So without another word, I hung up. And I haven't been able to stop thinking about her since.

Her curves. Her ski-slope nose. Her red lips. Her curls. God, her hair.

Now, call it fate or divine intervention, she is back in my world as a newly single woman.

And look, I know her mom is missing, and she's upset, yet unexpectedly, I'm happy.

Gingerly, she grabs the tissue from my hand. "Thank you." Her small voice, despite being in this dire situation, sounds like a song. I have to get myself under control. Finding Diane Sheridan is the most important thing. Not my unresolved feelings for her daughter.

She blows her nose, then turns her attention back to Denny. My hand reaches for her shoulder, but I pull back. "So what happens now?" she asks, with that old Rose bite surfacing.

"Maggie is your cousin, correct?" I ask.

She turns to look up at me, shocked that I knew this. "Yes, she is. And I'm as confused as you are that my mom would write that."

Denny sits down in the seat next to Rose, tapping the desk with his finger. "Ms. Sheridan, we need you to call Maggie. Once we saw the note today, we went to her residence to see if she would be willing to talk to us. She wasn't home."

Rose's eyes fly open. "Yes, she's in Italy. So you want me to call her right here, right now?" Confusion wraps around each word.

"Yes. Right now." Denny's answer leaves zero room for negotiation.

"Maggie had nothing to do with this!" she yells out, indignant.

Clearly this is agitating Rose, and I want to calm her since I hate seeing her upset. Why, I don't know.

Who am I kidding? I know why.

Pivoting from around the chair, I stand and face her as her intoxicating perfume fills my nose, making me unsteady. Using my desk for support, since my legs are now weak, I brace my hands on its edge. "We aren't accusing her of anything. Your mom wrote a note to you while in what was more than likely the darkest and scariest moment of her life. We don't know what was going through her head or what was happening when she wrote this. But it's our job to find out what she meant. And if Maggie's name is mentioned, then"—I shrug—"don't you think you owe it to your mom to find out?"

Rose lowers her chin, her jaw tightening as she fumbles in her purse. "I'm so confused. This makes no sense." She gets out her phone but hesitates. "I need a second."

Both Denny and I nod, staying silent while Rose processes. Finally, she refocuses on me.

"Is there anything specific I should say, or not say?"

Denny answers first. "Let her know where you are and who's with you and what we found. We will introduce ourselves and ask the questions. If she veers the conversation to you, don't ask why her name is on the note. Let her offer any information. Whether that be an explanation or denial. Got it?"

Rose nods and rests her phone down on the desk. Her lock screen pops up, and it's a photo of her and Niko. I scoff, but she hears it.

Her gaze snaps to me. "Give me a break. I haven't had a chance to change that yet."

Crossing my arms to hide the tightness that's forming, I sigh. They broke up, but she clearly isn't over the guy. My next words come out sharper than I want. "That's none of my business, Ms. Sheridan."

But, my God, do I wish it were.

We lock eyes for a moment, then she looks away, unlocking her phone and finding Maggie's number.

She slides the phone so that it's closer to me and Denny and then hits speaker as the phone rings. Maggie answers on the first ring.

"You're finally calling! What did the detective say?" Commotion fills the background.

"Where are you?" Rose asks. "It's like really late over there, isn't it?"

"It is! But Rose, the clubs stay open until like six a.m. over here. It's crazy. Katerina and I finally made it to the first bar. It's called La Maschera. You should see it!"

"Is that Italian for—"

"The Mask. Yep! And the guy I just met. Rose, he's so gorgeous."

Rose smiles, obviously happy for her cousin. "Nice."

"He's your typical hot Italian guy. Tall, dark hair, thick accent…"
Rose looks over at Denny as Maggie continues her description, and he
rolls his hand with a wrap-this-up gesture. Rose nods in understanding,
cutting off Maggie. "He sounds amazing, Maggie, but it's really important that I talk to you right now."

"Of course. Give me a second and let me get somewhere quieter."
The commotion fades gradually. "Okay, that's better. Sorry, I was
excited. Give me all the details. Did you give them hell?"

Rose winces.

Denny grunts.

I grin.

Rose continues. "Well, actually, they called me down to the precinct.
Someone found Mom's purse tossed away and hidden in the parking
garage of the Black Onyx. I'm here with them now, and they wanted
to ask you a few questions. They went to your house to talk to you in
person, but obviously, you weren't there."

"Okay. I understand. This is nerve-wracking, though."

Denny hinges forward, closer to the phone. "Ms. Colbert, this is
Captain Richard Dennison. Rose and I are here with Detective Cal
Masters. There's no reason to be nervous. We just have a few routine
questions for you."

Silence.

Denny's eyes flick me, then he continues. "Like Rose said, we tried
reaching you in person, but with you being out of the country, it's
important that we called now. We wanted to make sure we talked to
you sooner rather than later."

"I get it, but what does this have to do with me?"

Now it's my turn. "Ms. Colbert, this is Detective Masters. Along
with the purse, we also came into possession of a note Diane wrote,

we suspect, prior to her being abducted. It reads as follows." I read the note to her and watch as Rose sucks in a breath at her mother's words. "Now, I'm sure you understand this is raising some concerns."

"I get it. That is … strange." Her tone jumps an octave.

"Yes. Why would Mrs. Sheridan write to Rose asking her to tell you she's sorry, and she tried? Any ideas?"

"Hmm … let me think." She's quiet for a moment. "Could this have to do with wrecking her car last month? That's the only thing I can think of. What do you think, Rose?"

Rose peeks up at me, most likely for permission to answer. I nod. "I'm just as surprised as you are."

Denny comes in next. "Maggie, did you talk to Mrs. Sheridan before you departed for Italy?"

"I did. The day before I left for the airport."

"What was discussed?"

She sighs heavily. "Not much. She said how happy she was for me, and I could tell she was thrilled to send me on this trip. We talked about how Rose wasn't able to come and how that bummed us out." There's a pause. "She told me she loved me and to be careful and safe. The usual motherly stuff."

"Where was she when you spoke to her?"

"I have no idea."

I press some more. "Think hard, Ms. Colbert. Could you hear anything in the background? Did she say anything at all? Or was she with anyone?"

"All I heard was like maybe clothes rustling. It sounded as if she was getting ready for something. But the conversation was about me and my trip."

Denny purses his lips together. Rose still hasn't moved. Silence fills the room. "I need to get back to my friend. Is there anything else?" Maggie asks.

Denny clocks me with a look. We know what this means. The person being questioned is feeling defensive and trying to gain control of the conversation.

But, then again, being questioned by the police can make anyone jumpy and nervous.

Denny continues. "Ms. Colbert, we understand you are on vacation, but we may need to contact you again for further questioning. Please keep your phone with you."

"That's no problem. I want to help however I can. Am I allowed to ask Rose something?"

I shift; my boot lightly grazes Rose's foot. She relaxes. Her posture deflates as her breathing slows.

"Yes, that's fine," Denny replies.

"Thank you. Well, it's not really a question, but Rose, I forgot to tell you earlier that they had Orange Crush on the plane."

Rose stiffens, and her eyes whip up. "Orange Crush, huh?" she asks.

"Yep, it was amazing."

A code word. That's exactly what this is. It's completely out of left field, and based on Rose's reaction, I would bet my kidney that's what's going on.

Once again, Denny glares at me. He sees it too. "Alright, Ms. Colbert, like I said, make sure you are available." With that, Denny hits the red button, ending the call.

"You could have at least let me say goodbye," Rose accuses while aggressively grabbing her phone and shoving it in her purse.

Denny ignores this. "She mentioned wrecking your mom's car."

"Yeah, it was nothing really." Rose shrugs dismissively. "Maggie is a terrible driver, and one night, Mom, Maggie, and I were helping some friends decorate for their daughter's graduation party. They realized they hadn't bought enough wine, so Maggie volunteered to pick some up at the store. Her car was blocked in, so she took Mom's SUV instead. Well, she rear-ended someone while texting. Mom was pretty upset, to say the least, and they got into a massive argument. They both said some things they regretted. This wasn't the first time Maggie had been in an accident."

"Do you think that's what your mom was referring to?" I ask.

She shrugs again. "I mean, maybe. But they apologized and hugged it out the next day."

Denny gives me a side-glance and sighs. He knows she isn't going to like this next demand. "Rose, it's important that you limit contact with your cousin until we have a better grip on the situation."

She shoots out of the chair with her back to me, and of course, because I'm a guy, my eyes land on her butt. It's perfect, just like I remember.

Oh, my God! I need to stop! Which, in the presence of Rose Sheridan, is very difficult.

"She isn't involved in any of this!" she says in defiance.

"We aren't accusing her of anything." She turns and peers over her shoulder at me. As soon as her huge, gorgeous brown eyes meet mine, my knees almost give out. "However, your mom included that in her note for a reason. We need to figure out why."

Denny pulls out a folder that he's been holding. "Ms. Sheridan, Maggie's parents died in a house fire when she was twelve, is that correct?"

She freezes. "Yes. How do you know about that?"

He tosses it onto the desk. "This is part of the file from the night Maggie's parents died. Did you know your mother was there that evening?"

Rose's attention whips to Denny, disbelieve spreads across her beautiful features. "What?"

Denny opens the case file and fishes out a grainy black-and-white photograph. Rose picks it up, studying it. The photograph is of a house ablaze in the background. Firefighters and police officers are scattered, and dead center, looking at the house with her hand over her mouth, is Diane Sheridan.

With slow and deliberate movements, Rose's fingers grasp onto the photo. Shaking her head, she slowly sits. "I don't understand. She never told me she had been there."

She looks completely shocked and gutted. "What do you remember about that night, Rose?"

She steadies herself before starting. "Not much, honestly. I was only twelve years old. Maggie and I were at a slumber party. My mom came and picked us up in the morning, and I remember Maggie being confused because Mom wasn't taking her home. We went to my house instead. That's when Mom told her what had happened. We were so young. I don't think she fully grasped what transpired. She lived with us after that, and Mom became her guardian."

"Is that everything?"

Rose continues to study the picture. "I mean, we were kids. We helped Maggie cope with her grief, and then life soldiered on after that. School, growing up, boys. All the typical stuff." She sets the photo down. "I swear, this is all new to me."

I've done this job long enough to know if someone is lying. And Rose is not lying. Denny can tell as well. He has an interrogation persona he puts out there when he is trying to extract information from someone. But right now, he's softer. Kinder. It's a side of Denny I don't see much. But Rose has a way about her. She must have Denny under her spell as well.

"Well, this is all the more reason that finding your mom is our number one priority, and I know this may be hard, but limit your contact with Maggie."

Rose nods in agreement. "I understand."

Denny slaps his hands on his legs. "Okay then." He stands with purpose. "Cal, I'm going to send you and Rose to the Black Onyx. Check out the security footage. They finally got it ready for us after I decided to make this case everyone's problem. They were dragging their feet, and I was done. Talk about frustrating." He gathers up the photo. "Plus, check out the room she was staying in. The manager promised her room would remain untouched."

"Got it," I pause. "Wait, her room hasn't been searched yet? Why the delay?"

He continues. "You can blame me for that one. The Collins case has kept me busy these last two days."

"Denny, you should have told me. I would have …"

He raises his palm to halt me. "Later. Rose, stay close to Cal. Do as he says." He addresses me again. "I want hourly updates."

I salute him as he gathers up the file and scurries out of my office.

Rose turns in a flash to address me. "I'm driving separately."

I roll my head with a groan. "Did you not hear Denny? He wants us to stay together." I grab my keys from my desk. "Let's go."

"Nope. I'm driving myself." She starts to make her way out of the office, but I cut her off, slamming my hand onto the door frame.

Her glare reaches mine and, per usual, my stupid heart spikes. I can't stop staring. "Why are you so infuriating?" *And why do I like it so much?*

"Me? I'm infuriating?" she asks in disbelief. My jawline goes rigid as she shakes her head, explaining. "You have made it abundantly clear with your"—she waves a hand over my chest—"*body* language that you don't want me here helping. I figured I would do us both a favor and drive myself. You said it earlier; we have never been good at small talk. Right now, I need as much space from you as possible." She adds a final truth. "Plus, I need to be alone to process all this." She pauses. "Please."

I watch the words leave her red-tinted lips as her plea pierces through me.

I swallow hard. My hands clench.

A few things. She's not wrong. I have been rather curt with her, along with giving her the cold shoulder. Her mom is missing, and I need to show some more kindness.

But also, arguing with her, fighting, all the snark … I love it.

Probably too much.

The fact remains, if she were shadowing me again, and we weren't in the middle of an active investigation for her missing mother, I would have slammed this door shut and lifted her up onto my desk. Then kissed those ruby red lips until she was mine.

Geez, I need to stop.

Pushing off of the doorjamb, I wave my hand, gesturing for her to go. "Fine. But I'm following you there."

"Okay." She exhales, taking a step back.

"I'll meet you in the hotel lobby."

She waltzes past me, her hips swaying rhythmically down the long, echoing hallway. I watch. For much longer than I care to admit.

Rose Sheridan is back in my life.

I smile.

Chapter Six
7:45 p.m.

Rose

I sprint to my car, barely missing the torrential downpour. Slamming the door shut, I toss my purse onto the passenger side, and it's not until I sink into the seat that I can finally breathe.

My mother is missing, and just like before, Cal and I can't get along.

I yank the seatbelt across my waist and fasten it with a sharp click. "Get it together," I mutter to no one, because apparently, I've started giving myself pep talks now.

The car roars to life, and outside, the rain slams against the windshield in heavy sheets, blurring the world into shades of gray. And yeah, maybe I should've ridden with Cal. But honestly, it's probably for the best. I'm sure his car smells like him, and I'm not emotionally stable enough to handle that right now.

But ultimately, there's another reason I have to be alone.

Maggie.

Look, I know Denny said (more like demanded) for me to limit contact with her, but she used our code word.

Orange Crush.

This was always the word we would use in any conversation if we needed the other's help. Or we wanted to talk privately.

Once, she was out on a date with a complete loser. Those two words appeared on my phone screen in a text from her. I knew exactly what to do. So I called her, my voice full of fake fear and panic that Mom was in a car accident. I had just given her an excuse to leave the dreadful date.

You know, lies like that.

As soon as she said it, I knew she wanted to talk privately.

Cal's cruiser appears behind me, so with ease, I pull out of the station and onto the road. The wipers whip back and forth as the rain pounds the windshield hard and fast, blurring my view as they struggle to keep up.

Once I'm at the light, I pull up Maggie's number on my dashboard screen and hit call.

It rings only once. "Rose, what the heck is going on?" Her high-pitched squeal fills my car.

"I don't know, Maggie. The note Mom left me had your name on it, and of course that raises some questions." The light turns green, and I pull ahead as standing water causes my car to hydroplane slightly. I pause, gripping the steering wheel, swallow, and ask what I don't want to ask. "Maggie, why would Mom put that in the note?"

"I have no idea, and I wish I knew, Rose. I really do. You believe me, right?"

"That's a dumb question, of course I do. But Mom wrote that for a reason. I just really want to know why."

"Me too."

"I'm only trying to understand it all. Why did she want to apologize? You guys made up after the car accident, so it's not that." I'm rambling. "My mom was there the night of the fire. They showed me a picture."

"Wait. What?" A deep inhale follows the question. "They showed you a picture?"

"Yeah. Did you know? That mom was there?" I haven't the foggiest idea if I'm supposed to divulge this, but, come on. This is Maggie. My cousin. My best friend and my family. We tell each other everything.

There's a long stretch of silence, and I faintly hear rain falling. "I suspected."

I gasp, trying to keep my cool since I'm driving in a monsoon. "What? Maggie, why didn't you say anything?"

"Because I only thought it could be a possibility, and it doesn't really matter now. It won't bring them back." She sniffles.

"I'm sorry to dredge all this up."

"It's okay."

"Are you out with Katerina?" I ask, trying to change the subject. Again.

Cheering Maggie up. It's what I do best after all. Besides, I couldn't imagine being in a foreign country for the first time, and this is what I would have to deal with.

"Ummm ... no, I left. This is all too stressful. Plus, the jet lag has finally hit." She pulls in a tight, shaky inhale. "Do you trust this Cal?"

With the mention of his name, I glance in the rearview mirror, and he's gone. We must have gotten separated. Which is fine with me. He wasn't in the car with me, but he was too close. It felt like he was listening.

I stop at a red light as the wipers do little to help with my vision. Her question startles me. "I mean, I guess so. Why wouldn't I?"

"Think about it, Rosey Posey. You shadowed him last year. Did he know about the fire? He had to know, right? He never thought to mention that. And if he maybe knew Aunt Diane, did your name come up? I mean of course it did! I'm sure they looked into your mom. Her past and family relationships. He maybe should have mentioned all of this, don't you think? Seems shady if you ask me. Why did he withhold all of this from you?"

Huh, I hadn't thought of that. Maggie is right. And how much did he know about me on a personal level last year?

Doubt slithers under my skin.

Maggie continues. "Please be careful, Rose. Something's off about him. Then add in how he treated you the last time. I dont know … just some food for thought."

"You're right. And he's still being super combative. He doesn't want me here. At all."

"See."

I was, so clouded by everything that I didn't think about any of this. He may be the most infuriating handsome man I have ever met, but that doesn't mean I should trust him. "Thanks for always having my back."

"Ride or die. Always."

Chapter Seven
8:03 p.m.

Cal

I scroll aimlessly through my phone, standing near the hotel entrance that connects to the parking garage. The rain outside drums against the glass window, steady and relentless. I check the time again.

My gaze sweeps across the lobby, searching for her. Where is she? Somewhere between the traffic and the downpour, we got separated. Typical. And now, of course, my brain jumps straight to the worst-case scenario.

Did she get into an accident? Lose control in the storm? No. Don't go there.

I roll my shoulders, trying to shake off the unease tightening my chest. Just as I look at my phone again, a text buzzes across the screen.

Denny: Did you make it? The weather is something else right now.

Me: I've been here for ten minutes. She should be here by now.

Denny: Why didn't you ride together? I said I wanted her to be with you.

Me: She said she needed space.

Denny: She's calling Maggie.

Me: More than likely.

Denny: Find out if she did.

Denny: Actually, let me shoot her a text.

Me: No don't. It's dark and if she's still driving, I don't want her to check her phone. The roads are pretty bad.

Denny: Is that concern I sense?

Me: Shut up.

Denny: We both know that will never happen.

"I'm here. What now?"

Her voice slices clean through my text exchange, all clipped and impatient. I turn, and she's shoving her keys into her crossbody, rain still glistening in her hair. She looks … irritated. Or maybe that's just her default setting when I'm around.

"You made it okay?" I ask, genuine concern slipping through before I can help it. The roads were a mess, so she's lucky to have made it in one piece.

She blinks at me incredulous. "Um … I'm here, aren't I?"

"Oookay then." I draw the word out, biting back a grin. Yep, there's the Rose I remember. All sharp edges and fire. I can't really blame her for the extreme sass, given the hell she's been through lately.

I thumb out a quick text to Denny.

Me: She's here.

Denny: Keep your hands to yourself.

I scoff as I shove my phone into my back pocket and push off the pillar.

Typical Denny.

"Follow me," I say gruffly, slipping back into work mode.

She hesitates for half a beat, chin lifted, defiance written all over her. But then she falls into step behind me. Her shoes click against the tile in a rhythm that makes it way too easy to remember all the reasons she gets under my skin.

The Black Onyx Hotel is one of those hotels that practically drips with money. It's 1920s themed, stands twenty stories, and is the centerpiece of the downtown. You see the luxury the second you walk in through the revolving front entrance. Polished black-and-white checkered floors, gold trim everywhere, huge marble pillars that hit the ceiling. And staff that look like they've been trained not to blink unless a guest does first.

The lobby's packed tonight. People in tailored suits and glittering dresses are milling around, drinks in hand, like they've all stepped out of a Great Gatsby costume party. The low hum of conversation mixes with jazz streaming in from hidden speakers.

Front and center, a carpeted grand staircase sweeps up toward the mezzanine, the kind built to make an entrance. It gleams under a chandelier big enough to light up a city block. My eyes draw upward in awe to the second-floor balcony that frames the lobby, and to the hotel's secret speakeasy. Every inch of this place is gleaming like it's made to remind you that you don't belong here unless your wallet's thick enough.

And my wallet is definitely not thick enough.

I shift my weight, scanning the room. I've been in my share of high-end places for investigations, but this? This is something else. The kind of place where rich people pretend the world doesn't exist outside these walls.

Hotels like this aren't meant for people like me. They're meant for the ones born into it. The kind who can drop a few grand for a night just to say they were here. But tonight, I've got business to attend to. And no amount of gold trim or high-society polish is going to distract me from why I came.

Rose is completely unfazed. Walking through this—oh, I don't know, palace?—seems second nature to her.

We continue to stride in silence through the lobby and pass more marble than I have seen in a lifetime.

"So we'll start in security like Denny suggested," I start. "Look at the camera footage the night she went missing. I want you to look and see if you notice anything about how she was acting. Like maybe she knew the person."

"Fine."

I give her some major side-eye. She continues to walk with purpose, head held high, arms swinging. "Then we will look at her room, and see what happens from there."

"You're the boss," she scoffs.

That's it.

With two strides, I pivot sharply, blocking her path, preventing her from walking any further. She crashes into me, and I stare down at her gorgeous face. A face that looks like she wants to slice my throat with her nails. My heart quickens. "Do we have a problem?"

She gulps, showing her nerves, yet trying to act cool and unbothered. "Nope. No problem."

"Mm-hmm." I interlock my fingers behind my back. "I find it funny that after you talked to your cousin on the way over, your entire attitude changed." As my assessment dawns on her, I raise an eyebrow.

Her mouth drops. "H-how..." Her breath stirs. "How did you know I talked to Maggie?"

I close the distance, slow and deliberate. She stays perfectly still, not retreating. My traitorous pulse kicks up again. I tilt my head with a half-smile. "Orange Crush?"

She looks at the checkerboard floor. Busted. "Look. I know Denny told me not to talk to her—"

"For good reason."

"But that's our code word," she whines out. "We use it in desperate situations when we need rescuing or have to talk privately."

"Tell me exactly what you talked about."

She rears back. "What? Why? It was a private conversation."

I continue, irritation creeping in. "I get it. But, Rose."

For a fleeting moment, the badge, the gun, the chaos ... all of it falls away.

I'm not a cop anymore. I'm just me. Just Cal. Which always happens in her presence.

But I have to be professional.

"The fact remains that your mom used Maggie's name in a note that she wrote right before disappearing. Now, I'm not saying Maggie is a suspect, but it raises some questions. So for you to be having private conversations with her, well, it looks suspicious. We can't afford to have someone looking at you as a person of interest."

I let my words simmer for a second or two. She lifts her chin, and her gaze lands hard on mine, as sharp as glass. "She said I shouldn't trust you."

Punching me would have felt better than hearing that. Heat flares as I retreat a few inches, needing the space to breathe. "What else did she say?"

She ignores my question. "Why shouldn't I trust you, Cal?" she asks, clearly not letting this go.

"I want to hear why Maggie feels that way."

Her nostrils flare. "Why are you playing games right now?! My mom is missing, and you're acting like this is a joke!"

"A joke? My job, doing my job, is never a joke to me," I state sternly, attempting to keep cool.

Her temper flares. Something I remember seeing regularly before. And something that would always stir my blood. In a good way.

"Then tell me why I should trust you!" she shouts, the words echoing in the lobby. Now everyone's staring. Whispering. Pointing. "How do I know you won't sabotage things? Right now, I'm doubting whether you are capable of finding her because you won't talk to me!"

"Would you lower your voice?" I grit out. "The last thing we need is a scene. Let's take this to the garage."

She huffs and spins around, stomping in the direction of the parking garage.

I follow behind her as her arms gesture wildly. "Look, Cal. If you don't want to tell me something about my mom that you are clearly keeping from me, how am I supposed to work with you? Besides, I don't need you. I'll investigate this on my own with Denny and demand that he keeps you out of everything. Trust me, I have no problem doing that."

And I believe every word she's saying.

We've made our way back into the garage, and again, like before, this woman has my anger spiking into something hotter. *Why can't she work with me for Christ's sake!?* "Rose, would you stop, please?" I demand as I continue to follow her. The wind and rain howl outside while she searches for the keys, her fingers clumsy from nerves. The rain is shooting sideways through the open-air walls of the garage.

I scan our surroundings.

We're alone.

I grab her arm to stop her momentum. "Get your hands off me!" she yelps, trying to whip her arm away.

I catch her wrist and draw her toward the nearest pillar, guiding her until her back meets the cool concrete. My arms slam on either side of her shoulders, boxing her in. Not to intimidate her, but to make her see me, hear me. The space between us hums, charged and tight. Her breath catches, and mine does too. I need her attention, yes ... but God help me, I also just want her close.

"What did Maggie say?" The words scrape out of me like gravel. Her eyes dart up, startled, but there's something else there too. Heat, mixed with some confusion and the same current that's got my pulse in a chokehold.

Her chest rises as she sucks in a breath, pupils dark and blown. It's as if the question doesn't matter. Like the only thing either of us can focus on is this crackling energy that exists when she gets close.

And look, I'm aware this is completely unprofessional. But the thought of Rose having any doubts about me and my intentions toward her or this case is making me irrational. No woman's opinion has mattered to me like this.

"Why are you so close?" she rasps out, yet also not trying to get away.

I lower my chin, our faces inches apart as I zero in on the pulse in her throat, thumping away. "Do you want me to pull away?" I murmur.

The rain continues relentlessly and mimics the pounding of my heart. A slight gasp escapes her lips. Her mouth is a toe lift away. Big brown eyes pan up and tangle with mine, neither of us willing to break whatever this is. Our stares hold and strike with the same electricity that's coursing outside.

I hover closer and breathe the question once again. "Do you?"

What am I doing? I am on duty, and if this woman closes the gap, a millimeter, I will take her mouth as my own.

I've gotta pull back.

A streak of lightning flashes across the sky, followed by a roar of thunder, breaking us from this spell. We both jerk from the jolt of energy. I push off the pillar, and swallow hard, attempting to act like *that* didn't just happen. "Rose, I need you here with me. No one knows your mom better than you. And I promise you, if you tell me what Maggie said, I will be truthful with you."

There's a pause, her back still braced against the concrete. She mutters something under her breath that I don't catch. Then her eyes track to mine, full of questions. "Did you know my mom was there the night Maggie's parents died?"

"I did."

"Did you know a year ago?"

"Yes." My arms hang limply at my sides. "Yes, I knew."

There's a sudden tense inhale, like this moment is stealing something. Her frown causes a sharp pain in my chest. "You should have told me! I thought we had someth—" she confesses, hurt, yet stopping her thought from releasing. I know what she was going to say. She thought we had something.

We did.

Until I messed it up.

"It wasn't intentional, Rose. You shadowing me and what happened to Maggie's parents were two separate things. That is still an open investigation, albeit a cold one, so no, I didn't share any details with you. I only knew so much anyway because that case was turned over to Denny about two years ago when the previous captain retired, who, I might add, was a crappy investigator. Denny is still playing catch-up from all that guy missed. I helped Denny weed through the cases that took priority, and unfortunately, that wasn't one of them. Names and a few details were all I had. Plus, I assumed you knew the story of that night. Why wouldn't you? She's your mom."

She stands there, staring at me, blinking, taking in everything I said, so I continue, the words tumbling out of me, rushed and messy. "Then your mom was taken, and the case landed on our desks. It took us a few days to connect the dots, but then it clicked. We only skimmed the file from the night of the fire. We saw the photograph and wanted to talk to you and Maggie first."

I take a moment to compose myself and slow down. "I was so upset for you. I wanted to reach out so badly, but Denny advised against it. It would have been too personal."

Man! Why did I just say that?

"And you're always a professional, aren't you?" she bites out, throwing my words back in my face—the excuse I used right after I pulled away from our kiss.

That one stung.

I ignore this and proceed, "Is that why Maggie told you not to trust me? Because I withheld that information from you?"

She nods.

"I see," I mutter as she turns from the pillar, sending a bit of gravel skittering across the pavement as thunder rolls overhead.

With a deliberate step, I move closer until her eyes meet mine. "Believe me, Rose," I implore. "Not once did I lie to you. There were things I couldn't say. Couldn't talk about. Things I didn't even know myself. But I *never* lied."

She exhales, the turmoil draining from her face. "That makes sense."

I stare. Longer than I should.

And there it is again. The same look she had given me the night in the bar. The one that burned straight through me then ... and still does now.

Because, God, she is beautiful. She doesn't pull away as my breath seizes. "Don't leave," I plead. "Let's find your mom. Together." Her eyes stay locked. "And maybe not try to kill each other in the process."

She chuckles as the rain pelts the walls while I wait for her answer. Her shoulders relax. "I will always be honest with you, Rose. Lying to you isn't an option."

She barely breathes and whispers her answer. "Okay."

We make our way back to the lobby, and Rose is lighter now as we walk.

I really should have told her to leave. And I definitely shouldn't have told her I almost called her. So stupid. Being around her is testing my sanity.

I squeeze my eyes, attempting to compose myself.

Which is why I don't see the body until I run straight into it.

Oomph! We collide. "Oh geez. Sorry, man."

The guy in the three-piece suit jolts back a step or two. "No problem…" Then he looks over my shoulder as a sudden recognition fills his face. "Rose?"

Her head pops around my body. "Niko?"

You can't be serious? Did I bodyslam into Rose's ex?

This is just my luck.

Rose pivots around me, obviously in quite a hurry to get closer to this dude. Jealousy erupts, and I don't like it.

Reluctantly, they both go in for a hug. It's awkward, but I don't miss the small smile that crosses Niko's lips as soon as their bodies connect.

I look away.

"W–what are you doing here?" Rose asks, sounding almost excited.

Niko raises a mask. "My company is hosting a Gatsby-themed masquerade ball. Remember, we were supposed to go together?"

This captures my attention as I look around the lobby again. The throngs of people milling around in elaborate costumes now make sense. Some are wearing masks, which I didn't notice before.

This type of crowd is a cop's worst nightmare. Identities hidden away. It's easy to commit crimes when no one knows who you are.

Rose fiddles with the hem of her shirt. "That's right." She shuffles her feet. "How have you been?"

He smiles. Again.

On instinct, and since I refuse to admit I'm jealous, I scan over my competition. He's not as tall as I am. Maybe an inch or two shorter, yet still towers over Rose. His hair is blonde, slicked back in a rich-bro kinda way.

I mean, I'm not blind. He's a good-looking dude. I understand what Rose saw in him.

"I've been good. No complaints here. I have a lot on my plate right now, which is keeping me busy." Rose nods as he turns his attention to me. His face falls as his jaw tenses. "And who might you be?"

I extend my hand. "Detective Cal Masters. I'm investigating Diane Sheridan's disappearance." His palm wraps around mine, and with all his strength, he squeezes.

A chuckle bubbles forth at this guy's attempt to intimidate me. I swallow it down.

He's funny.

I squeeze. Harder. "You're Niko, I assume?" He drops his hand, flexing it once, then twice. Probably from the pain.

I grin.

"Oh, sorry!" Rose reenters the chat. "I should have introduced you. Niko is my ex."

"Ah yes. The guy from the screensaver on your phone." Rose twists slightly, her eyes narrowing in warning. Niko grins, clearly pleased with this revelation.

But his irritation returns. "So you're here with him. Helping? *Togeth-er?*" Niko grinds his teeth.

"Yes. Like he said, Cal is investigating my mom's disappearance." She pauses to compose herself. "It's been so hard, Niko."

Why is she being so vulnerable with him? And with me, I get nothing but sass and attitude.

I need to stop with this jealousy.

Niko's face falls. "I'm so sorry you are dealing with this, Rose. I loved your mom, you know that."

She gives him a tight smile and sniffles. "I know."

"I figured you must have been pretty stressed when you didn't re-spond to my text earlier. Do you need me to tag along? I can h—"

"That won't be necessary," I snap, rougher than I intend. Rose's gaze snaps to mine, sharp and full of fire, but I hold it anyway. Our stares lock, maxed out on anger and frustration. Niko doesn't flinch—his eyes stay trained on her like I'm invisible.

She addresses him again. "Actually, I had to have special permission to be here, so I doubt that would work. But it's sweet of you to offer."

"You know I would do anything for you, Rosebud."

With that nickname drop, I decide to leave these two love birds and let them talk. Gently, I rest my palm on her lower back.

Inappropriate? Yes.

Necessary? Also yes.

Niko's eyes immediately zero in on my touch. "I'm going to be at the front desk asking about security. Take your time."

Reluctantly, I walk away, but also watching.

Something about this guy rubs me the wrong way.

Call it a cop's instinct that comes from years of watching people, reading the things they don't say. But there's a vibe coming off him. And it's not a good one.

Or maybe I'm just a paranoid SOB.

While I'm waiting for the clerk to pull up the information I asked for, Rose breaks away from Mr. Wonderful with a hug and walks in my direction. She moves with purpose, her eyes focused on mine, worry etched across her face.

But it's not her that Niko watches as she comes my way.

It's me.

Chapter Eight
8:28 p.m.

Rose

A ll I want to do is find my mom. Is that too much to ask? Instead, I am being forced to spend time with Cal.

The one that got away. The one that drives me up a wall.

And now I've run into Niko.

The one that broke my heart.

What are the odds, honest to God?!

Cal, of course, looks constipated as I approach him. "Did you find out if we can talk to security?"

"They are getting someone now. It's late, so who knows what kind of guards work the night shift," Cal answers, his scrutiny still on my ex. I turn around, and Niko disappears down the hallway leading to a different set of elevators. One that will take him to the upper floors where the event center is.

"So, that was *Niko*?" Cal inquires, curious and, honestly, he sounds a little jealous.

"Yep. That was Niko." The ex I stupidly jumped into a relationship with because the man standing in front of me rejected me.

Cal leans against the counter. "For an ex, he sure seems overly concerned about you," he bites out.

I glance back toward where Niko had been standing, a strange feeling curling low in my stomach. I wish I understood what the hell these feelings even are. Everything's a tangled mess lately. My mom, these men.

"He is," I say finally, quieter than I mean to. "He always was. Which makes our breakup that much more confusing."

Cal's brow lifts. "He didn't give you a reason?"

I let out a dry laugh that sounds way more bitter than I intend. "Not really. He called me out of the blue one Sunday afternoon right before we were supposed to leave for lunch with my mom and broke it off."

Cal's head jerks up. "He broke up with you. Over the phone?"

I nod. His reaction shouldn't please me as much as it does, but the disgust on his face almost feels ... satisfying. But it's also weird that he's pretending like he gives a crap.

"Did he at least say why?" he presses.

"That's the thing," I say, switching into a mocking imitation of Niko's voice. "'I love you, but I can't be with you anymore.'" I roll my eyes. "I think he was cheating. He'd been acting weird for weeks, secretive. Then—poof." I shrug, forcing a little laugh that feels like sandpaper in my throat. "I'll probably never get any answers."

Cal doesn't respond right away. When I finally glance at him, he's studying me, really studying me with that steady, too-serious gaze that always sees too much. My defenses immediately go up.

"What?" I snap, crossing my arms. "Don't look at me like that."

"Like what?" he asks.

"Like you care," I shoot back before I can stop myself. Because he doesn't care. He left me.

"Rose." My name on his lips is a plea. Not Sheridan. But Rose.

"Okay, Detective," the hotel clerk breaks our connection. Cal jerks away from me, turning to the employee with his cop personality flipped back on. "The head of nighttime security will meet you down in the basement lobby. Take elevator three down to the ground floor, and he will be there."

Cop Cal answers. "Thank you very much. I appreciate your time."

The young lady instantly blushes and then scurries away.

He turns to regard me, soft Cal returning. "You ready for this?"

I nod. "Let's go." But am I? Ready?

No.

With his usual swagger and long strides, Cal marches down the lobby toward the elevators. The noise and low conversations of the crowd fill our silence as we walk in tandem.

This hotel is so huge it requires three sets of elevators. Huge brass numbers hang above each one.

Elevator One, the one Niko probably took, leads to the upper event centers and restaurants. Set number two is for the rooms. Number three takes you to the ground floor and parking garage.

Cal pushes the button for Elevator Three, and as we wait, a heavy hush settles around us. The door dings and opens as we step inside, silent. We both turn to face the doors. He presses G for ground.

We stand not talking, descending lower, when Cal finally speaks. "He's an idiot, Rose." My eyes snap to him as he continues to look straight ahead. "If I were lucky enough to have a woman like you ..." He never turns to me but continues with a quiet kind of ache. "I would never let you go."

The doors slides open, leaving me more confused than ever.

But I smile anyway.

A bald man with a full beard, wearing what looks like a mall cop uniform and nearly as tall as Cal, greets us just as the clerk promised. He extends his hand. "Cal Masters?"

Cal takes his hand. "Yes, and this is Rose Sheridan."

He turns to me, shaking my hand. "Michael Hawkins. It's a pleasure to meet you both."

His lips purse briefly. "Please know I'm so sorry about your mother, Ms. Sheridan. I promise I will do everything I can to help with the investigation."

I smile. He seems kind and genuine. "Thank you. I appreciate that."

He turns back to Cal. "And please accept my sincerest apologies for the delay in getting the footage. We've been having issues with our servers, and there were quite a bit of hoops we needed to jump through."

Cal tilts his head as a small grin appears, obviously impressed. "Thank you. I'm sure you understand, time is of the essence."

"I do. So let's get started. Follow me this way." Cal glances at me, lifting his eyebrows. Mr. Hawkins guides us down a long, narrow hallway that feels like it hasn't seen sunlight in a century. It's tight, musty, and the kind of creepy that makes goosebumps crawl up my neck. A far cry from the opulence we just left in the lobby. I fold my arms around myself, shivering as our footsteps echo off the walls.

And when I say long, I mean long. This hallway could give airport terminals a run for their money. Based on the cracked concrete and ancient pipes, you can tell this place has been standing for over a hundred years.

Cal keeps glancing my way, reading my nerves without a word. Somehow, just having him here makes the dark feel a little less cold.

Finally, Mr. Hawkins turns sharply, and the corridor dead-ends into a massive steel door. We nearly walk right into it.

He taps the badge hanging from a lanyard around his neck, and a huge clank and buzz sound. He pushes it open.

A wave of loud, sharp, and organized chaos smacks me in the face the second I step inside. My pulse spikes. This place doesn't play around. The security here is intense.

Cal and Mr. Hawkins move through it like they belong here, slipping into the room with that easy confidence of people who have worked in this world for years. Meanwhile, I'm rooted to the doorway, wide-eyed and motionless, attempting to take it all in.

Everything's bigger, louder, and more real than I expected.

I shrink back, very, very out of my depth.

The hum of fluorescent lights and the whoosh of a fan fill the space. A sterile noise only amplifies the dread tightening and coiling every muscle in my body. An entire wall of monitors fills the far wall, casting a blue glow. Mr. Hawkins sits stiffly at a desk in the far corner, his attention immediately focuses on his computer screen, clicking through menus. Cal hovers over him.

I stand unmoving and silent.

"Sheridan, why don't you pull up a chair?" Cal asks. He turns, no longer feeling my presence at his side. Panic floods his face as he frantically scans the room, searching for me. He finds me still standing at the entrance, a statue in the doorway.

In a flash, he's right beside me. "Hey, are you okay?" The question comes out soft and caring, and immediately, I relax some.

I look up at his towering, yet peaceful figure. "Yeah, this is ... a lot. And overwhelming. Maybe it's just a sensory overload. I don't know. I thought I was ready, but now, seeing all of this ..."

His hand reaches out, but then he retracts it, clenching his fist. I chastise myself because I really wish he hadn't. "I'm here every step of the way. If it's too much, look away. No pressure. I promise."

An appreciative smile crosses my lips, and I nod. It's when I finally step forward that his palm, open and wide, rests on my lower back, guiding me.

That touch, that one touch, propels me forward. To my mom.

As soon as we make it to Mr. Hawkins's desk, Cal gestures to the chair. I sit. He has everything cued up and ready to go. "This is from three nights ago," Mr. Hawkins mutters, tapping away on the keyboard. "Garage Level A."

As Cal gets closer to the monitor, his broad frame blocks part of the screen. "Level A is the basement level, correct?" he asks. Mr. Hawkins nods.

Cal, steady and in control, begins barking out commands. "Run it from ten minutes before the timestamp we gave you. But not too fast that we would miss anything."

The footage flutters, then plays. Rows of concrete pillars stretch across the grainy frame, cars lined like shadows beneath harsh fluorescent lights. For several seconds, nothing moves. My stomach churns, waiting.

And then she's on the screen.

She appears in the far corner of the monitor, moving fast, her heels clattering against the pavement, slowing her down. Mom is a runner. She would run marathons for kicks and giggles. I'm sure she didn't expect to be running like this.

She clutches her purse like it's a lifeline, head jerking side to side, as though she knew, or felt, someone closing in.

My hand trembles, hovering, wanting to touch the screen. Tears threaten to spill over, but I push them down.

"Mom," I squeak out, inching closer to the screen.

Cal leans into me, only a centimeter, but my body registers it.

Then she disappears, the feed cutting to the same location, yet slightly different.

Seconds later, the screen shutters, and she appears again.

"What was that?" Cal questions.

Mr. Hawkins doesn't tear his focus from the screen as his hand hovers over the mouse. His eyebrows scrunch together. "I don't know. It seems like the video was tampered with, maybe. Like I said, server issues. It's been going on for a couple of weeks."

"Who would do that?"

Mr. Hawkins shrugs, perplexed. Cal grunts, but I tune them out as I watch Mom break into a desperate run, sprinting past parked cars. A figure appears behind her. Taller, dressed in dark clothing, the face obscured by the hood of a sweatshirt and a ski mask. His pace isn't frantic, but steady.

Deliberate.

Hunting.

Bile coupled with desperation rises. "Oh, God … oh, God, Cal, he's following her."

The feed continues to flip between images. The scene with my mom's chase and the one without. Cal doesn't speak, but I feel the shift in his body beside me, coiled up tight. His jaw flexes, focusing on the screen.

"Slow it down," he barks out with an icy calm.

Mr. Hawkins obeys, adjusting the playback. The video staggers forward frame by frame. Mom, frightened and with hair spilling across her face, glances behind her. In the next frame, her heel catches on the pavement, and she stumbles, palms slapping the ground, before trying to scramble back up unsuccessfully. One of her heels is now broken.

I gasp, my hand flying to my mouth. "She fell—"

"She's trying to get back up," Cal reassures me quickly. It's wild because what I'm seeing on screen, happened three days ago. Watching it now, though, it seems like it's unfolding in real time.

The man in the hood doesn't falter. He moves around a pillar, not rushing, not losing ground. He's a good eight car lengths behind her.

"Zoom in," Cal orders.

The manager hesitates. "It'll get blurrier, and with the feed acting up, I don't—"

"Do it."

The screen magnifies, edges fuzzing with static. The mask still hides the man's face, but his posture is unmistakable: shoulders squared, arms swinging loosely at his sides.

Unfazed.

Confident.

Ruthless.

My breaths come in heavier and labored, so I press my palm against the desk, desperate to have something solid to hold on to. "Why isn't anyone there? Why isn't anyone around to help her?"

Cal doesn't answer; his sole focus is the video. I watch helplessly as Mom crawls to a pillar, trying to conceal herself. Then she crouches between two black SUVs, vanishing from view.

Cal points to where my mom disappeared from the screen. "This is where we found the note." The hooded man slows, tilting his head, scanning. His lips are moving, but the video is silent. He gets closer, weaving through the rows.

My nails dig into my palm. I lean forward, wanting to be closer to her. Wanting to help. But I can't. "Run, Mom," I beg. "Please, run." I know there's no way she can hear me, but I plead anyway.

And then static.

The picture fractures, a burst of black and snow tearing across the screen.

What the?!

"No!" I screech, slamming my hand on the desk. "Can't … why … how … what happened?" None of my words forms a sentence.

Mr. Hawkins is already typing, the clicking of the keyboard loud in the silence, but the screen remains dark, unyielding. "That's … that's all it recorded. Don't know why it cut out. It could be our current issues or maybe the system rebooted. It's been doing that lately."

My vision blurs with tears. "Rebooted? Are you telling me it conveniently shut off the second my mother …" I'm ready to crack. "The second she needed someone to see?"

Mr. Hawkins shifts. "Could be a glitch. Power surge. It honestly could have been anything. We have been scrambling to find answers, let me tell you."

Cal straightens, his presence filling the room. "Or someone made sure the feed went dark," he states low, deliberate.

I turn to face him. I'm so desperate for someone to understand how I feel. And I know he will. "She was right there, Cal. You saw her. He was right behind her. And then—" The words catch as I press both hands to my face.

Hundreds of scenarios feed my anxiety about what could have happened to her.

None of them are good.

Cal reaches out, hesitates, but thinks better of it, his hands falling to his side.

"We'll find her," he says, each word carved in stone. His eyes fly to the blank screen, unblinking, hard with resolve. Then they lock with mine. "I promise."

"What happens now?" I ask as Cal's resolve stays steady, and it keeps me from vanishing right along with my mom.

"It's time to search her room."

Chapter Nine
9:17 p.m.

Cal

The hallway on the twelfth floor reeks of bleach and cheap disinfectant, the kind that clings to your throat. We move in single file through the navy blue and dark green decorated floor, passing room after room. Triangular shaped retro lights hang on the walls, adding a soft glow to the hallway. We sidestep a maid's cart abandoned against the wall, confirming my worst fear.

They've already cleaned the room.

I am going to kill Denny. Why wouldn't he send me to do this before today if he was busy with another case? It's really unlike him to miss something like this.

Rose walks behind me, and every step she takes feels heavier than the last. I want to reach for her, to promise I'll find her mother and take this fear away, but all I can do is keep moving forward. The look on her face back in that security office gutted me. She was lost, trembling, and trying so damn hard to be brave. It still sits in my chest like a bruise.

I glance over my shoulder. She's scanning the hallway, her expression tense, eyes wide and wary. She's holding it together, but barely. So I decide to talk some, hoping it will ease her anxiety a little. "If your mom lives close by, why did she book a room?"

She shrugs, still taking in her surroundings. "Mom doesn't like to drive at night and it was just easier. The conference was going to keep her pretty busy. This way she could come back to her room and nap in between lectures. She attends these every year and they wipe her out."

"Makes sense."

"This is it," Mr. Hawkins announces, stopping at room 1243. He swipes the keycard; the light flashes green, and the lock clicks. His hand moves for the handle, but I stop him, my instincts kicking in before he can turn it.

"I got it," I demand.

Opening the door, I step aside to allow Rose to enter first with Mr. Hawkins behind me, and of course, the room is picture-perfect ready. Fresh linens. Vacuum tracks in the carpet. The bathroom counter gleams like a showroom.

Every room in the Black Onyx is tailored to the theme of the whole hotel. The Roaring 20s. And money. Lamp shaded gold sconces hang on the walls. Navy blue and gold art déco architecture wallpaper covers the main wall. The massive leather headboard of the king-size bed almost reaches the ceiling. Green velvet chairs rest around a dark mahogany table. Black and white photographs of flapper girls adorn the walls. It's rich and expensive.

And spotless.

These maids are good at their jobs, that's for sure.

Instantly, I'm full of fury. Yeah, Denny should've been here earlier, but either way, they were told not to clean the room. As my luck would have it, that message didn't make it to the maid staff.

This has to be a joke, right?

Dead center of the room, Rose freezes, astonished, shoulders sagging. She looks as if someone punched her in the gut. "Where are my mother's things?" she asks.

I turn to address Mr. Hawkins. "That's what I would like to know. What happened? My superior, Richard Dennison, called with specific instructions for this room to remain untouched until our arrival to inspect it."

Mr. Hawkins is scanning the room in a panic. "I ... I don't know what happened. This isn't my department, so I'm in the dark like you guys. It's upsetting, to say the least." He holds up a finger and walks back to the door. "One moment. Felicia!" he hollers as he stands in the hallway, holding the door open. A woman, a maid, who I assume is Felicia, scurries over. "This is Felicia, the night maid. She does one final inspection of the emptied rooms for the next day's check-ins." He addresses the maid, "Felicia, please pull up the room cleaning assignments for the day." She nods and pulls out what looks like a company-issued phone.

She scrolls, then hands it to Mr. Hawkins. "Here are the rooms on this floor scheduled for today. Plus the ones I'm assigned to double-check for tomorrow."

He scans it, shaking his head. "Wait here," he commands as Felicia stands staring wide-eyed while the door closes on her. Poor thing probably thinks she's done something wrong.

He hands me the phone, pointing to the screen. "This report makes zero sense, but if you look right here"—he points to a list of room numbers—"for whatever reason, this room is listed among the cleaning assignments. Clearly, someone dropped the ball. But I will get to the bottom of it."

"Please do," I bark out as I hand him back the phone. "In the meantime, wait in the hall. We will need you to escort us to where her things are once we are done here."

"Yes, sir." He nods and hands me the key. "If you need anything else, please let us know. Take your time." I watch as his dejected figure disappears through the door.

It clicks shut, and I'm already scanning, taking in every detail. Rose continues to stand motionless, her shoes making imprints in the carpet, watching me intently. As much as I love having her near me, no matter the situation, I need her out of my way so that I can think.

"Sit down, Sheridan. Let me handle this," I bark out as I open and close dresser drawers.

She turns; the fire in her eyes is unmistakable. "Sit down? Not happening. I know my mom and what to look for."

I guess sassy Rose is back. It's true, I adore this version of the woman, but she's not who I want her to be right now. I clench my jaw. She doesn't get it. She *couldn't* get it.

"Look," I implore firmly. "If there's something here, it'll be hidden and subtle. I know what I'm doing."

Her chin lifts, stubborn as ever. "You don't know my mother like I do."

Damn it. She was right.

But that didn't matter. This wasn't about knowing her mother. This was about knowing the evidence.

"I'm not doubting the relationship you have with your mom, but you're very emotional right now, and rightly so. Emotions cloud judgment. You'll miss what's in plain sight. Besides"—I glance around the room—"it's spotless. I doubt we will find anything."

Her nostrils flare. "And you think ..." She stops, composing herself. "You think you're not emotional?" she snaps. "Don't act like you're made of stone, Cal. I know better. We got drinks. Remember. Or have you forgotten that night? Because I remember. Especially how it ended." Her face twists, and the wound from my rejection is still fresh.

Oh, I remember all right, Rose.

There is no doubt she's been holding this in since she arrived today. She knows I let my guard down with her that night. And she remembers how I left. And based on the daggers she's shooting at me right now, she's hurt.

This cuts deeper than I expect. I can't face her. Too much of a coward to face the hurt I caused her. I focus on the desk. The drawer slides open with a hollow scrape and then closes on its own. It's empty and spotless. I run my hand along the bottom.

"Stay put. Please," I say without looking back. I can't. My emotions have to stay in check, and when I look at her, Detective Cal Masters becomes a lovesick teenager.

She huffs and drops onto the bed. I hear the defiance in the movement, like she was doing it just to prove she wasn't obeying me. Even though she did.

I search quietly, yet I know she's watching me. And she's nowhere near ready to let this go.

"You almost kissed me. That night. You walked me to my car, held me, and then … left. It was humiliating."

I freeze. My fingers curl around the edge of the closet as heat coupled with guilt surges through me.

She continues. "For months, I thought I had done something wrong. Then, I told myself it didn't matter. Like, maybe I imagined the whole thing." She puffs out a small chuckle. "But I didn't imagine it, Cal. You were there. You looked at me like you wanted it too, and then you didn't."

"That was a mistake."

"A mistake?!" Her tone is sharp and daring. I squeeze my eyes shut. That was probably the wrong thing to say. What I meant was, it was a mistake to stop. But I don't say that out loud.

She pauses. "Or you don't want to admit you wanted to kiss me?"

I turn, my gaze meeting hers, and the world pauses. She has no idea what she is doing to me. "It's not that I wanted to stop it. I pulled away because it was wrong. Bad timing. We were working together. I wasn't about to cross that line."

"Maybe I didn't want you to stop," she volleys, cutting me to the bone.

My pulse kicks up hard. Without realizing it, and in only three steps, I'm so close the warmth radiating off her seeps under my skin.

"You don't know what you're saying," I rasp. Our knees touch. She raises her hooded eyes, her hands clenching the down comforter. "We're working together again. And if I cross that line now..."

"You're saying you don't want to?"

God help me.

I want to kiss her again more than anything. For almost a year, that almost-kiss was all I thought about. I didn't expect to run into Rose Sheridan again. Then someone up and took her mom, and here we are.

As soon as she showed up at the precinct this afternoon, it was like no time had passed. She makes me feel things no woman ever has.

My hand flexes uselessly at my side, aching to touch her. I inch closer, breathing her in. "You don't know how much I want to. But it's not appropriate. Not here. Not now."

Hurt whizzes across her features before she quickly buries it under anger. She shoots off the bed, standing so that we are somewhat at eye level. "So you get to decide for both of us? Again?"

That stung worse than a knife. And she's not wrong. I did choose to stop things that night. Then, for the three weeks that followed, I pushed her away with rudeness.

I'm drawn to her like a magnet that's too strong to pull away from. The second her eyes meet mine, all reason frays.

But I step back enough to breathe, shoving the emotion down, rebuilding the armor she keeps breaking through. "I'm trying to do the right thing here, Sheridan." And pulling away is what I have to do because I know what's happening. Rose is trying to distract herself from the pain and uncertainty of the real reason we are here.

Her mom.

And it's pretty obvious she is using me as that distraction. Granted, under different circumstances, this attention from her would send me over the edge.

Hell, it is now. But I have a job to do.

"Maybe I get to decide what's right for me," she says with conviction.

I sigh and ignore her, turning back to the search, each movement sharper, harsher.

Don't stop searching.

Don't stop searching.

Don't stop searching.

We stay silent. Her eyes drill into my back as I check the closet, the nightstand, the edges of the carpet, under the bed.

Nothing.

Nothing but the echo of what we aren't saying.

Finally, she breaks. "You're doing it again. Pushing me away. And what? Do you think that makes you noble, Cal? A gentleman? You think keeping me at arm's length will keep me safe from you? Your job?"

I hate hearing the tremor in her question. It strips away all my excuses.

I straighten and face her. "Fine, you want the truth." She doesn't break contact as once again, I step to be closer to her. "If I let myself get distracted, I'll miss something that matters. And your mother doesn't have the luxury of my losing focus." She's now studying the patterned carpet beneath her feet. I lift her chin, and our eyes lock and seize. "Because trust me, I want to get distracted."

She gasps.

My pulse is pounding in my ears as my whole body coils tight with restraint. "It's about both of us," I say, quieter now. "Because if I give in, I won't be able to stop."

Her breath stumbles, and the charged silence around us practically vibrates.

I swear under my breath, and every instinct inside of me is fighting itself.

The pull to kiss her is so real and strong. But if I do, it's over. Each line I drew would disappear. And there'd be no coming back.

So I retreat back again, dropping my hand, trying not to sound rough. "We can't do this. Not now. Not while your mother's life might depend on us keeping our heads straight."

Her lips press into a thin line. She turns away, shoulders stiff. Yep ... too rough. "You're right," she admits. "I hate saying that. But you are."

Both of us stand there, not speaking. Only feeling. Knowing acting would destroy us. The silence is worse this time.

Thick.

Final.

I go back to searching the room with hands that won't stop shaking, telling myself over and over it was the right choice.

But I'm lying.

Her back is to me now, arms wrapped around her body.

She sniffles.

Damn it. She's crying.

"You're upset," I say, softer, trying to understand. "You're scared for your mom, and I don't blame you. But that's all this is. That's why you're looking at me like that. I've seen it before. You're trying to push down the fear you have about your mom by pulling in a different emotion. One that makes you forget and feel good."

She turns, eyes flashing. "How do I keep looking at you?"

"Like you want me to cross a line I can't return from." I hate that I'm falling apart at the seams. "I won't do that, Sheridan. Not when you're hurting. I won't take advantage of you."

She looks at me, intently, breathing hard. Out of nowhere, she stomps her foot, and her gaze burns hotter. "Stop it!"

"Stop what?" I chuckle at the sudden change in her mood. God, I love her sass. My pulse hammers.

"Stop being right." She's steadier as she continues. "But just because you're right, doesn't mean I don't want this."

Frustration (both mine and hers) courses through us.

The seconds tick away.

I feel.

I feel so damn much when I'm with her.

We don't smile.

We don't blink.

We only stand and stare.

She on one side of the room. I on the other.

If she was trying to strip me down with her words, it was working. My jaw locks as every muscle turns to stone.

Every part of me aches to go to her, but I force myself to hold back. I have to. "I want it too," I admit, the words dragging out of me. A piece of her hair falls, and all I want to do is tuck it behind her ear. "But wanting this and acting on it are two very different things."

Her lips curve, faint but knowing. "For now."

I smirk as thoughts of where this hopefully will go in the future play on a loop in my mind. "For now."

I look away, forcing myself back into motion, checking the night-stand again, though I know it's empty. Anything to keep my hands busy. Anything to keep from grabbing her, pulling her in, and giving her what she is asking for.

The silence stretches again, but it's not cold this time.

It's alive.

A hot current we both desire, no matter how much I try to ignore it.

And God help me, I didn't know how much longer I'd be able to.

Because the truth is, the case isn't the only thing on the line. If I slip and gave in, I wouldn't just lose focus. I could lose her. And I wasn't sure I could survive that.

Not again.

***

After the room search proved fruitless, we leave and meet the night-time manager in the lobby, Mr. Hawkins still in tow. The manager's expression tightens, hands clasped like he wants nothing more than to be anywhere else.

I don't care. This is ultimately all their fault, anyway.

As soon as we approach him, he starts. "Housekeeping has already processed the room," he says, apologetic but clipped. *Tell us something we don't already know.* "Personal items were logged and secured, per policy." He pauses, waiting for me to reply. I don't. He clears his throat. "Please accept my apologize for the mix-up about the cleaning of the room."

I grunt, ready to respond, but Mr. Hawkins beats me to it. "Well, I will hold you personally responsible if this mistake costs this investigation time and evidence."

This Mr. Hawkins has my vote. The manager lowers his head and nods.

Rose stiffens beside me. Anger rolls off of her in waves. "Where?"

The manager hesitates, knowing they royally screwed up. "In storage. We keep guests' belongings for thirty days unless instructed otherwise."

"Let's go," I blurt out, my tone leaving no room for negotiation. And before Rose explodes.

The manager nods quickly. "Right this way, sir. Mr. Hawkins, I got it from here." The security manager, whom I actually like now, has to leave.

I extend my hand to the man. "Mr. Hawkins, thank you for your time."

He takes it, smiling. "You're welcome." Then he directs his next words to Rose. "Ms. Sheridan, I truly hope your mother is found alive."

Well, hell, now I like him even more.

She nods, smiling. "Thank you."

Don't you worry, Rose. I will find your mom.

After exiting the busy lobby, we enter elevator one and endure a painfully uncomfortable ride to the twentieth floor. The very top of this massive place. He leads us down a service corridor, away from the ballrooms and restaurants that I'm sure offer an amazing view of the city skyline.

However, this part of the hotel is cold and unfeeling. The walls here are bare, the air chiller, the hum of fluorescent lights harsh against the silence. Rose walks close, her hand brushes against mine once, accidentally. Or maybe not.

We reach the end of the hallway as the manager unlocks a steel door and ushers us inside. The storage room is nothing glamorous. There are rows of shelves. Each with neatly tagged bags, boxes, and suitcases, waiting for their owners.

"This section." He points to the middle shelf. A black plastic tub rests on the wire shelf, sealed and labeled with her mother's name.

Diane Sheridan.

Rose moves first, stretching up on her toes toward the box like it holds a piece of her heart. As if her mother might somehow be waiting inside. Before I can stop myself, I reach over her head, standing behind her, my arm brushing hers. The soft contact sends a jolt through me. "Let me get it," I murmur, lower than intended.

She turns, her face just inches from mine. For a breath, neither of us moves. Her eyes meet mine, raw and tangled with grief and something unspoken. The weight of it hits me square in the chest. "I'll process and catalog everything first," I say gently, forcing my voice steady. "Inspect it all. Then, when I'm done ... you can look."

"Okay," she whimpers out and steps back.

Then, I address the hotel manager. "Leave us."

"Yes, sir." He scurries away. Normally, I'm not this gruff, but these people royally screwed up with the room. Who knows what could have gotten thrown away or swept up. So, my desire to be nice is over.

Heaving the large bin from the shelf, I place it on the steel table behind us. Rose rounds the other side, watching me intently.

"We'll go through everything," I say firmly. "Piece by piece. If there's something here, we'll find it." I yank rubber gloves from my pants pocket and slide them on. I open the lid and peer inside. It's only her suitcase. Rose stands craning her neck to get a better look. "When I pull out the suitcase, can you put the bin on the floor, please?" She nods, doing as instructed.

Slowly, I pull at the zipper. *Zzzttt.* The sound echoes throughout the small space. Inside are the ordinary scraps of a person's life. Clothes. A book. A pair of reading glasses. A phone charger coiled neatly. All the things that should have felt familiar but here feel hollow.

One by one, I photograph each piece with my phone and search the items, hoping, for Rose, that I find some kind of clue.

But there's nothing.

After about twenty minutes of work, I step back. "Okay, you can look if you want."

Rose's eyes meet mine, silently asking permission. I nod. "Go ahead." Slowly, she pulls out a silk scarf, touching it, smoothing it along her fingers. She tries to hide the sharp inhale. But I caught it.

When it comes to Rose, I see it all.

"They just packed her stuff away like this." Her voice breaks, and I hate the helplessness clawing at me. "Like she's ... gone."

She glances at me, searching. And for a split second, the fight from earlier in the room is gone. All that's left is trust.

Fragile, dangerous trust.

Rose lifts the silk scarf again, pressing it to her face as if it might still hold her mother's scent. Her shoulders tremor.

"I hate this," she mumbles.

I swallow hard; the words caught. "She's not gone. We don't know that yet. And besides, they were only doing their job. These things don't mean anything to them."

Her eyes dart up, sharp and wet all at once. "Then why does it feel like it?"

It's true; this is Rose, which makes this more personal, but it's also like any other case. And the same emotions and questions always come to the surface regarding to victims who are left behind. I don't have an answer. Not one that wouldn't sound rehearsed. So instead, I reach into the suitcase, pulling out a paperback with a cracked spine, and hand it to her. "Because you care. Because it matters. That's why it's so heavy."

Her fingers brush mine as she takes the book. The contact is small, fleeting—but it burns through me all the same. She doesn't pull away immediately.

"You always do that. Even before," she murmurs.

"Do what?"

"Make it sound like you're giving me logic when, really, you're giving me comfort."

My jaw clenches as I look away, attempting to build that wall back up. "I'm not here to comfort you, Rose. I'm here to help you find your mom."

"It's possible to do both, you know," she retorts softly, almost tender.

I don't respond. My chest aches with the truth. She isn't wrong.

After setting the book down, she reaches for her mother's glasses, the lenses reflecting the light. Her hand trembles. "She can't see without these."

Her words break apart, tearing me in two. "We'll find her," I promise, steady and certain, though a small piece of me fears making promises like that to families. It's a promise that sometimes is impossible to keep.

And I want to keep all the promises I make to Rose. At all costs.

She looks at me, eyes shining, and right now, the room feels too small. The shelves, the dim light overhead, the weight of the case—it all fades. It's her and me, tethered by something we shouldn't touch but can't seem to cut away from.

I want so badly to pull her against me and kiss her until the world outside this storage room stops spinning.

I'm completely lost.

Lost in her magic. Her words. Her way.

Just her.

I inhale a breath full of nothing but Rose. But I have to let go. For today, this is as close as I would get to her.

She blinks, looking down at the suitcase again, and I force myself to remain steady. "Let's pack this all back up. There's nothing here, unfortunately."

But the truth is, my mind isn't on the evidence anymore. It's on her. Always on her. And I wasn't sure how much longer I could keep pretending otherwise.

"Do you have to take her stuff, or can I?" she asks, small and delicate.

I stare at her a moment too long before checking myself. "Let's leave it here for now, and I'll text Denny to have someone come and pick it up."

She nods, her arm brushing mine as we reach for the zipper. That tiny spark of contact lingers longer than it should, a reminder of everything we haven't confessed in the hotel room.

I shove the feeling down. The case comes first. It has to.

With my resolve firmly intact, Rose's butt starts to ring.

Chapter Ten
10:15 p.m.

Rose

The silence stretches, and I can't bring myself to look at Cal again—not without the risk of saying something I'll regret.

The past hour has been a whirlwind of emotions. Mostly embarrassment, if I'm honest—after the way I practically threw myself at him in that hotel room. And he was right. I was desperate to feel *something* other than fear and find comfort in anything that wasn't chaos.

In that moment, everything changed.

Then I saw my mom's things, and it hit me harder than I could've ever prepared for. A wave of emotion crashed over me, sharp and unexpected. I tried to keep it together, to swallow it down and mask the ache building behind my ribs.

The need to always appear strong is something I have to let go.

Smelling her on that scarf and touching her things made all of this feel so real.

But it wasn't only that. Not for me.

Being around Cal today reminded me how much I still want this. *Us.*

And yes, I've given him attitude and sass, but it was all a way to keep him at arm's length.

Because honestly, I didn't think he wanted me.

But then it was the little things I noticed. First, in his office, picking up on my nerves. The jealousy of seeing Niko with me. His determination to find my mom. His confession that he almost reached out when he got my mom's case. I've seen the fleeting moments of concern that flash across his face when he looks at me.

And let's not forget the way he guides me with his hand on my back.

All of it was showing me a very different version of Cal than the one I concocted in my head.

Then came my mom's room and his confession. It's been replaying in my head ever since.

Because trust me, I want to get distracted. I almost fainted.

We hit pause, sure, but that look—the same one from that night at the bar—was still there. The kind that says everything words can't.

I wanted to reach for him, to stop him from running again.

And maybe, when all of this insanity finally ends, we'll get that chance. A real one this time.

And despite everything that's happened ... all the danger and doubt, part of me still believes that he's worth the risk.

All of these thoughts cause something inside of me to stutter when my phone buzzes in my back pocket, cutting through the silence.

I jump at the sharp and sudden noise as Cal looks away, shoving his hands into his pockets.

I pull my phone out of my jeans and glance at the screen, startled. "It's her."

Maggie.

Cal's head snaps up. "Put it on speaker," he barks quick and firm. "Don't answer on video. And don't tell her you're at the hotel or that I'm here."

I frown. "I ... I don't understand. Why?"

"Do it, Sheridan." His tone leaves no room for argument.

"Geez, I see grumpy cop is back," I mutter under my breath. And why do I like the grumpy version of Cal so much?

"Trust me. This isn't grumpy."

"You mean he gets grumpier?" The phone continues to ring.

Cal presses his fingers to the bridge of his nose, the muscle in his jaw ticking, clearly irritated. "For God's sake, just answer the phone." He looks at me again, the irritation softening. "*Please.*"

A crack of thunder erupts outside, adding to the mood in the room.

"Fine." I draw myself upright, trying to steady my anxious body. Holding the phone out, I swipe and hit speaker. "Maggie?"

"Rose." Maggie's answer is tight and full of urgency. "Finally. I've been trying to call you. So do you have an update?"

Cal gives nothing away, only folds his arms while squinting at the phone screen.

"You called me in the last hour? My phone didn't ring."

"I did! Maybe it's the whole international call thing." I flinch at her shrill, high-pitched reply. "I'm freaking out over here. Stuck in stupid Italy. Please say you have something."

Cal stands motionless, concentrating on me and Maggie, his face like stone. "I don't have much to tell," I reply carefully. "We're … still looking." I cringe at how easily the lie slipped out. Cal nods. I guess that was the right thing to say. I pick my nails because I don't enjoy withholding information from Maggie. This is fresh territory for us.

She exhales, sharp and frustrated. "That's not good enough. Are they doing their jobs? We have to find Aunt Diane!"

Cal's eyes narrow, not liking Maggie's accusation. "Of course they are. It's not that simple."

"Of course it's not simple, but keeping me in the dark like this isn't cool."

"I'm not intentionally keeping you in the dark, Maggie. There's nothing to tell. When I know something, you will be the first person I call, I promise."

There's a pause, then her next question hardens. "Is Cal with you?"

This catches me off guard, and I hesitate, unsure how to answer. He stays still, but the tightness in his jaw gives him away. Then he gives a small nod. Silent permission to tell her the truth.

"Yes," I reply. "I'm still working with him."

"I see." Another harsh inhale through the line, then: "Did anything we talked about earlier sink in? You can't trust him, Rose. You can't. God, you're so stupid."

I stop breathing. *She called me stupid.* I'm frozen, caught between disbelief and the urge to defend myself. Cal's focus, though, is solely on me.

He's waiting. Waiting to see if the doubts that Maggie tried to plant in me earlier took root.

They didn't.

We lock eyes, and in them I find the strength to answer her. "Maggie, *don't* call me stupid. I heard you earlier. I did. But Cal has been nothing but kind, helpful, and honest with me since this started. I have every reason to trust him. He explained his reasons for withholding information from me, and I believe him."

He tries to hide it by turning his head away, but his lips upturn into the slightest smile.

She huffs in disgust. "And you actually believe him? Or is this something more? Admit it. You're happy to be around him again, aren't you?"

"Yes, I do believe him." I grin. "And I trust him, Maggie. One hundred percent." Cal's face softens. "And yes, I do like being around him again." His smile stretches from ear to ear. I haven't seen that megawatt smile since that night in the bar.

"I honestly thought you were smarter than that, Rose."

The line goes dead.

I lower the phone slowly, staring at the dark screen.

Cal's next words fill the empty air and slice through the shock coursing through me. "What was that all about?"

I mull over his question, doing my best not to let the sting show. "That's just Maggie," I murmur. "She doesn't like being left out." Sliding my phone into my pocket, I add softly, "But she's never hung up on me before." My throat tightens. "Or called me stupid."

He studies me, arms still crossed, his expression flat. "Sheridan, that wasn't her being pushy or wanting to be in the know. There was more behind it." Now, it's his turn to pause. "And you're not stupid. In fact, I think you're brilliant."

I let the compliment sink in, loving and real. "Thank you."

"Talk to me. Why did she react like that?"

The words catch, but I force them out. "I honestly don't know. That didn't sound like her. At all." A sudden sadness fills me.

Something shifts in Cal as empathy flashes on his face. "We can hurt the people we care about the most, sometimes."

He says this like he's speaking from experience. We lock eyes, and he gives me a tight smile. As though he is admitting something he's too afraid to say out loud.

That's what he did. He pushed me away. And he regrets it.

I glance away and continue. "That conversation. That wasn't Maggie. Something is wrong. She's the carefree one. Always happy. The effervescent, quintessential party girl that people gravitate to and want to be around. She exudes such fun energy that it's hard not to want to be in her orbit." A soft quiver leaves my lips at the description of the woman I love like a sister.

"Well, when people deal with trauma, they overcompensate this way. It comes out in their personalities. And your mom being missing is traumatic for both of you. But just because you are handling it so well, doesn't mean she is. She's halfway around the world, probably feeling helpless. That can be a lot to deal with," Cal reasons.

"You're probably right." I ponder his words. I'm sure she feels helpless and alone. That's all this is. She's lashing out. When we talk again, she'll apologize.

He nods, and I have to admit, his being here with me is helping. "You think I'm handling this well?"

Cal comes around the steel table. He's standing next to me now, resting against the metal, staring at me. "As well as you can be." My breath hitches slightly. "You feel lost, helpless and full of fear. You are the type of person who needs things to make sense. And none of this makes sense or is easy to explain. Which is tearing you up inside."

I don't know how, but this man sees me. And I think he always has. "How do you know what I'm feeling?"

He exhales, studying the scuffed tips of his boots while he crosses his ankles and thinks. When he finally lifts his head, the air shifts. His gaze pins me, steady and unflinching. Then his words split me open. "Because I like being in *your* orbit, Sheridan."

I'm stunned into silence. *Nope, no words are formed after that confession.*

He pauses, then saunters around the table again, like he's fighting his own thoughts. And quickly changes the subject. "Tell me about her childhood. What you know of it." He heaves the tote back up and onto the shelf it was on prior.

I pick at my nails to do something with my hands. "Um, Maggie grew up poor. Her dad couldn't hold down a steady job, and her mom didn't work. I'm not sure why." Memories begin to flood back into my mind. "My mom would offer to help them, financially I mean. And they would always refuse. Mom and Uncle Pete had a complicated relationship. I think there was always some resentment there."

His eyebrows pinch together. "How do you mean?"

"With money. My mom does well at her job. And my dad's family was well off, so when my dad passed away from cancer when I was only eight he left everything to her. I think my uncle always hated that. He was the type of guy that felt like"—I lift my fingers and air quote—"'I don't have money, so no one should.'"

"That had to be stressful." He wipes his thumb over his lip, taking this in. "Do you think that leaving her home and losing her parents might have caused some resentment? Towards you and your mom? Kinda like, 'you have your mom but I don't.'"

I know Cal means well, but this is out of the realm of possibility for Maggie and me. We are joined at the hip. A dull ache forms with nowhere to go. "No. Absolutely not," I hiss while clutching the scarf then wrapping it roughly around my waist. "She lost her entire world that night, Cal. And my mom, our home—it became hers, too. We've been inseparable ever since."

He studies me. "So how close are you, really?" he asks, treading lightly.

Surprise flares at his question, making me feel defiant. "Close enough that she knows what I'm thinking before I say it. Close enough that when she's scared, I know it. And right now? She's terrified. That's all this is. So if you're implying something else ... don't."

His jaw tightens, like my answer raises more questions than it settles.

Chapter Eleven
10:40 p.m.

Cal

We leave the storage room with nothing but Rose's mother's scarf, now tied around her waist, and a heaviness that neither of us wants to name. It's from this insane chemistry charging the case.

And us.

"Let's hit security one last time," I tell Rose as we walk to the elevator. "And download everything. I want to rewatch it again and make sure we didn't miss anything. Plus, Denny will want to see it." She says nothing, only nods, her eyes distant. The usual Rose spark is gone. I would take the banter we had a year ago—hell, minutes ago—over the sullen version walking beside me right now. My heart aches to find her mom and put a smile back on her face again.

On our way back to the elevators, the muffled pulse of music drifts from one of the event rooms. The doors are thrown wide, decorated with one of those obnoxious balloon archways. Light and laughter spill into the corridor. Guests glide in and out, glittering flapper dresses brushing against sharp Prohibition-era suits. Jeweled masks hide half their faces.

Rose slows, drawn to the glow like a moth to a flame. Her gaze lingers on the entrance. "That's the masquerade ball," she says softly. "Niko's in there. I should …" She swallows, hesitation threading through her. "Say goodbye." Her teeth catch her lower lip, and then her eyes flick to mine, silently searching and asking.

Oh, hell no is what I want to say. But I don't.

I bite back my initial reaction. I do not want to see this dude again. Or worse, see *her* with him.

She's seeking him out. And that thought stirs something ugly deep inside me. "Now?" I squeak out. So much for trying to hide it.

She turns, her lips twitching with the ghost of a smile. "It's polite, Cal. He was kind to me when I saw him earlier. Concerned about me and my mom."

I should tell her no and remind her that we don't have time for polite goodbyes. But the look in her eyes, and the slightest pout that's pushing out her bottom lip … damn it. I exhale through my nose and nod. "Fine. Make it quick."

We enter the party as an attendant hands us masks at the door. I set mine aside instantly. "Not happening."

Rose laughs softly, slipping hers on her face, the silk ribbon trailing against the soft, supple skin of her cheek. "What, don't want to play along?" she nudges me. "Always no fun and so serious all the time."

"I'm on duty," I mutter while scanning the room.

The ballroom looks like something out of a dream. The second we step inside, I understand why people pay ridiculous money to stay here.

Gold light spills from chandeliers big enough to blind you, reflecting off the marble floors like liquid fire. Drapes stretch and hang from the ceiling. Every inch of the place is dripping with old-world glamor. Black and gold accents, tall arched windows, and velvet curtains framing the view of the storm outside. It's like Jay Gatsby himself is going to emerge from the crowd.

The air hums with jazz coming from a live band that plays near the stage. Couples in masks spin across the floor. Sequins, silk, and feathers shimmer while champagne flutes clink. Laughter echoes.

For a second, it almost feels like time stopped in here.

Everyone's masked, which makes it worse somehow. Nobody's who they appear to be. It's elegant, of course, but this isn't my scene.

Rose nudges me again, trying to capture my attention. I tear my eyes from the ballroom and look at her. My breath catches. The way the mask frames her face. The way her baby browns glitter and sparkle beneath it.

I'm completely captivated.

She smiles while fiddling with the ribbon in the back. The mask keeps slipping down her nose and cheeks. "How do I look?"

Stunning.

Gorgeous.

Breathtaking in every way.

But I don't say any of those things. "Like you're ready to party."

She turns. "Can you adjust this for me? I'm all thumbs, and it won't stay tied."

With her back facing me, my eyes instantly draw to the line of her neck and her exposed shoulder. Up close, her skin isn't flawless. It's real, freckled, tan, and without trying, makes her more beautiful. A strawberry birthmark, small and delicate, peeks out from behind her top.

I wonder what the rest of it looks like.

On a shaky breath, I focus on my fingers and the satin ribbon as I form the bow. Her curls tickle my wrist while I tie the knot, and for a heartbeat, I forget why we are here. The faint lavender scent from her shampoo fills my nose, and I breathe it in. In order to keep my fingers from shaking, I pull the ribbon tighter than I need to. Because if I don't, I might let them wander and trace the curve of her neck or the pulse beneath her skin.

When I'm done, I linger a second too long, her hair still tangled in my breath.

"All done." My hands fall to my sides.

She turns, touching the mask and ribbon, making sure it's secure, oblivious to my inner freak-out. "Thank you. You ready?"

To find your ex so you can see him? No, Rose, I am not ready.

But I follow her anyway as she leads us deeper into the party. She's scanning the room as we weave through the crowd. My eyes? Only on her.

Then she spots him. "There he is," she quivers out with a hint of excitement and a huge grin. My gut churns as I watch her look at him like that.

It was only a smile. Don't panic.

The lie tastes bitter.

Casually, he's reclining on one of the high-top tables, holding a glass of wine, chatting it up with a gaggle of women. They all burst out laughing at something he's saying. Niko must be a funny guy.

Whatever.

He downs a swig of his merlot as he looks around the room. Niko zeroes in on Rose right away and grins the moment he sees her. "Rose." The dude's face lights up like a freaking Christmas tree. He immediately abandons his harem.

Before I can intercept, she's in his arms, hugging him like ... like she wants it. I grind my teeth, shutting down the desire screaming to pull her back.

"I wanted to say goodbye," she mutters into his body.

Without letting her go or her letting him go, he glances at me. "You guys are leaving?"

I guess he's asking me. "Shortly. I might be back if we find something."

"I'm so scared, Niko," she mumbles into his chest.

He continues to hold her, then kisses the top of her head. "I know. I'm so sorry." She draws her eyes up to meet his. "If you guys are done, you can stay here with me, the way we planned. I just want to help. Or maybe we could leave and go back to your place. You shouldn't be alone."

My fingers dig into my palm.

Rose pulls away, and disappointment flashes across Niko's face. She looks at me sheepishly. "I better not."

Niko's hand trails to her arm and squeezes her biceps. "Do you have a few minutes? I would like to talk to you in private right over there." He points to the darkened area directly behind us. "It will only be a minute. I have so much to say, and I miss you, Rose."

Not happening.

He will have to kill me before I let him take her anywhere. Especially down a dark hallway that looks like it leads to nowhere. The dude is delusional.

Does that make me sound like a caveman? Yes.

But I prefer to call it 'doing my job and protecting her.'

I'm pretty sure half the ballroom can hear my jaw clenching over the music. Back in the hotel room, every look she gave me said, 'Come closer.' I thought what I saw in her eyes was want. We took it a step further and made a promise to push pause on what was happening. But then she sees Niko, and suddenly, that same look is pointed at him.

A cruel truth hits me. Hard.

They've got a history. I can see it in the way they move around each other. As if there's something unfinished that's still lurking. And the worst part?

If I hadn't been such a damn coward, that history could've been mine.

As I'm about to put the brakes on this whole reunion, Rose makes up her own mind. She steps back from Niko and sidles next to me. "I can't, Niko. Cal and I are heading back to the precinct to report back what we found here. Finding Mom is my priority. Sitting around wallowing and crying isn't going to bring her home. I have to keep searching."

Another word: bye.

I relax as soon as she steps away from him. I don't let it show—at least I try not to—but the relief hits hard and is impossible to hide. My chest puffs out.

Niko nods in agreement. "Of course. I understand. If you need anything, please call me, okay? Help with the case or anything. Day or night. I mean it."

Internally, I'm laughing at this idiot because if he cared so much, he wouldn't have let her go in the first place.

Kinda like I did. But that's neither here nor there.

The moron keeps talking. "It's important to be realistic, Rose. This probably isn't going to end well, and you'll need someone," Niko says smoothly. Sounding as if he cares.

She stiffens yet offers him the same genuine smile she always does. But there's a strain beneath it. The kindness in her eyes doesn't quite reach the edges. She doesn't like his negativity; it unsettles her.

"I will," she says softly, yet trembling enough to betray her nerves. "But Cal *will* find her, Niko. And if I cry, it'll be from joy. Not sadness."

Her gentle words carry a sweetness laced with conviction.

She's right. *I* will find her. For Rose.

"No, yeah, of course. You're right." He extends his hand. An invitation. "I hope I didn't upset you."

She doesn't take it. "No. You didn't."

I've had it with this guy. My patience snaps clean in two. "Time to go," I say, the words coming out harsher than I intend.

Rose shoots me a glare sharp enough to cut glass.

She turns back to him. "Bye, Niko," she says.

"Goodbye, Rose. Take care of yourself."

Niko glares at me, smug as ever, before waving Rose a lingering goodbye and melting into the crowd. She waves back and watches him until he's gone, then spins on me as she whips off the mask and flings in onto a nearby table.

"You didn't have to be such a Neanderthal."

Yeah, I did.

Her accusation stings, but I don't bite. Instead, I turn on my heel and head for the exit, jaw tight, pulse still pounding. "We need to go," I bark out because walking away is easier than saying what I really want to—that watching her with him drives me out of my damn mind.

She's right behind me when I've barely made it halfway through the crowd. Her voice catches me.

"Cal, wait."

I stop. Turn. She's standing next to a high-top table, looking smaller somehow, her confidence stripped away. Her arms fold across her chest like she's trying to hold herself together. "What if he's right?" she whispers.

Her question comes out of left field. "About what?"

She hesitates, then meets my eyes. "That I need to be realistic. That … maybe we won't find her. What if she's really gone?" Her voice trembles, cracking in the quiet. "The footage didn't give anything away. There were no clues in her room or her things. This hotel showed us nothing. Nothing. And every day that passes …" She trails off, shaking her head. "I can't stop picturing what might be happening to her."

Something twists deep in my chest. I can't stand seeing her like this—torn apart, scared, doubting everything. Plus, I want to wring Niko's neck for planting these thoughts in her head.

"Rose," I say softly, and before I can think better of it, I close the space between us and pull her against me.

For a second, she freezes, arms hanging limply at her side, breath hitching. Then her body gives in. She presses into me, her hands wrap tightly around my waist, her forehead tucked under my chin. She's shaking as I hold her tighter, ignoring the part of me that screams I shouldn't.

"Hey," I murmur into her hair. "We're going to find her. I promise you that. I won't stop until we do."

She exhales shakily against my body; the sound breaks something inside me. The scent of her hair, the warmth of her pressed against me—it's all too much.

Too good.

Too dangerous.

And that's when I realize I've crossed a line I can't uncross.

I force myself to let go, stepping back before I forget why I shouldn't. Her eyes flick up to meet mine, wet and searching, and for a moment, neither of us says a word.

Neither of us breathes.

We stare.

We yearn.

We want.

"Let's get going," I finally manage, trying to keep my voice level.

She nods, but her gaze lingers on me, steady and unspoken, like she knows there's more behind my words than either of us is ready to face.

Chapter Twelve
11:01 p.m.

Rose

D ing!
 The gold elevator doors open as Cal waves his hand over the ornate arched entrance, giving me permission to enter. He follows me in, and we end up on opposite sides of this small box. He pushes L for lobby, and I'm staring at the marbled checkerboard floor, not wanting to look at him. Needless to say, things have gotten super awkward.

And I don't like it.

These feelings that I have had since the day I laid eyes on him are mixing and fighting with the sorrow I'm experiencing.

The doors shut, and the dimly lit elevator begins its descent to the ground floor and lobby. Soft melodic music fills the small space. I have maybe seconds with him before we enter the world once again. And then part ways. More than likely, Denny will be the one I talk to when it comes to my mom's disappearance. If there is any news or a break in the case, since he is the lead detective, he will call me. Not Cal.

How I want it to be Cal. So badly.

My attention travels to the digital floor countdown above the sliding doors.

19

Beep.

18

Beep.

17

Beep.

16

Beep.

We are whizzing down this shaft faster than I want. Silence descends, heavy and absolute. Every beep mimics the beating of my heart.

His eyes are on me. I know it. Eyes full of nothing but concern.

A heaviness settles in my belly, knowing our time is almost up. I can't help myself. I never could when I'm with him.

14

Beep.

12

Beep.

I drag my eyes to meet his. The music, the movement, the space … it swirls until there is only him.

As our stares collide, his concern morphs into something else entirely. His intensity, now heavy and unguarded, drags over me like a touch, and I feel it everywhere. Neither of us moves.

But there is something.

Something that's inevitable and too late to stop.

An electric charge. As if the lightning outside has made its way into this elevator.

"Rose." My name rolling off of his tongue, deep and meaningful, fills my chest.

11

Beep.

10

Beep.

"Yeah," I reply.

9

Beep.

8

Beep.

7

Beep.

In less time than it takes to breathe, he crosses the five feet of space that separates us and stops inches from me. I clench the handrail behind me, bracing myself. He's so close. But not close enough. He cups my face with his hands.

5

Beep.

"We only have a few seconds left," he says, low and gruff as his thumb grazes my cheek.

"You'd better make them count, then."

Holy smokes, who am I? Please tell me I didn't just say that. Lust-filled Rose is on a whole other level.

My eyes drift close.

4

Beep.

He pulls my face to his.

His breath drifts over my skin as his lips part.

I'm waiting, wanting, needing.

THUD!

Without warning, the elevator surges, jolting us. Cal braces me, grabbing my waist and pulling me to him. Creaks, grinding, and groans surround us as the lights cut out once, twice, three times. My adrenaline spikes trying to figure out what is happening. Without warning, we are plunged into darkness.

We aren't moving.

The music stops.

Silence and pitch black inkiness surrounds us as Cal's hands grip me, holding me with such a protective force that it almost hurts.

My body ignites with awareness, each breath tighter than the last as panic begins to rise.

"Cal. W … What's happening?" I whisper. As if there is anyone else in here with us to hear me.

"The power probably went out. More than likely from the storm."

When I say it's pitch black, I'm not joking. I have no idea what he's doing, but he's fidgeting as his body shifts. He's looking around. I think. Looking for what? No idea.

But he doesn't let me go.

"Oh, my God! Are we stuck here?!" My voice goes from a whisper to a full-blown shrill in seconds.

I haven't had a panic attack since college. Years of frequent therapy sessions and medication have helped me to pinpoint when one is starting.

But nothing in all my years of therapy has prepared me for this. Stuck in an elevator. During the worst storm this area has ever seen. And to make matters worse, I've always struggled with claustrophobia.

I can't breathe.

"It's okay. These systems have a small power backup that comes to your rescue when there is an abrupt power failure like this. It should kick on any second," he counters, so sure. So strong.

We wait.

And wait some more.

Still waiting.

Nothing.

His hands release me. "I don't understand what is going on. It should have happened by now." Cal reaches for his phone, turning on the flashlight. He shines it on the control panel.

But without his presence grounding me, my breathing spikes. In-stinctively, my hand shoots to my heart, clutching my chest, the erratic rhythm hitting my palm through my shirt.

"C-Cal," I call to him as my back slides down the wall, the handrail scraping my back. My mind is telling me the space is shrinking. It's going to swallow me whole.

He's still studying the panel, waving his phone around, inspecting it from all angles. "Where is the dang call button at?"

His illuminated silhouette blurs.

"I'm going to call the front desk. To let them know we are trapped in here."

I watch his mouth moving as he talks into his phone, but the words float over me, mixing together and making no sense. I draw my legs to my body and hug my knees.

Why is this happening? Why are we stuck in this box, dangling, with nothing but a faulty system in control? *And why did I just think about that?!*

The air in my lungs disappears.

"I-I can't br-breathe." I don't know if it is the desperation in my voice, or perhaps the words themselves that seem to jolt him from his search. His focus whips in my direction.

"Geez! Sheridan." Within a second flat, he drops and crouches before me, setting his phone on the floor beside him. The flashlight shoots straight upwards.

He brushes my hair away and then points to his face with two fingers. "Eyes on me." An intense, shadowed green stare glares back at me. He's focused, in control, and steady.

"Deep breath in." With my focus solely on him, I do what he says. "Now hold it for seven, six, five, four, three, two ... now exhale. Eight, seven, six, five, four, three, two, one."

My heart slows as he grabs my hands, his thumb running circles along my pulse. "We are in this together, okay?"

"O … Okay," I strangle out.

A small, satisfied smile plays on his lips. "Let's do that a few more times. You with me?"

I nod like a bobblehead. "Yes."

And as promised, he stays with me. Centered. Helping me breathe. Although we're trapped in this elevator, and I'm mildly panicking, along with his touch and soothing voice, I know I'm safe. Cared for. And cherished.

"Better?" he asks.

"I am thank you." Well, sort of.

"Okay, good." His thumbs continue moving, his eyes sweeping softly over my face. "I'm going to go back over to the panel and see if there's anyone else we can call. I talked to the front desk but I want everyone to know."

As I'm about to tell him, 'Do what you can to get us the heck out of here,' the elevator plunges sharply.

I screech. It drops only inches, but feels like a mile.

The jolt causes Cal to drop to his knees, while also grabbing hold of me. "Cal. I can't do this! We are going to die! This isn't—"

His attention is back on me. "It's gonna be okay."

I'm hysterical now, shaking my head wildly. "It's not! This box is going to plunge to the ground, and our bodies will be splattered all over these walls."

"That's an unpleasant thought." Amusement crosses his lips.

"Cal! I'm serious!"

"I have no doubt."

"You have to help me!" Panic claws at me as I desperately scan the surroundings, searching for a lifeline. Everything is more intense. The darkness, the gold handrail, the light from his phone. All of it is swallowing me whole.

"What can I do? Tell me." His whole expression changes when he sees how serious I am. But there is only one thing I need.

My lifeline.

Him.

Him close to me again with his arms around me, his chest up against mine, I want his lips—

Then it hits me.

"Kiss me."

His head jerks back. "What?"

"Kiss me. Now." I reach for him, but he grabs my wrists, stopping me.

"I am *not* going to kiss you now. We have to get you calm—"

"Do it."

He drops my hand and backs away. "No."

"Yes. It will work. A distraction."

"NO! I'm warning you, Sheridan."

"Do it! Or so help me God, I will tell Denny that you left me panicking on the floor and did nothing to—"

"Oh, screw it."

Faster than the bullets in his gun can travel, his lips are on mine.

And Oh. My. God.

I wanted this, yet was completely unprepared. This kiss is unlike anything I've experienced.

Ever.

My breath, stolen. The world—being trapped in this box—forgotten. As his mouth moves over mine, the world narrows to his breath, his pull, and the quiet hum of my feelings. A hum I know now only he can stir. When he finally pulls back, I'm breathless, trembling, and everything inside me relaxes.

With a swift movement, he sits, pulling me close against his hard body; my skin tingles from his touch. We connect, stare, and share a silent understanding.

There is no doubt we both want the same thing.

Before I can stop myself, I straddle his lap, as the heat of his body zips through me, melting my anxieties away. His hand curls around my head as his fingers thread through my curls, tugging gently. "I love your hair," he breathes out.

I'm pretty sure I'm going to black out.

Then, he hesitates, his eyes lingering on my lips, a rush of anticipation in their depths before leaning in. "Rose," he says against my mouth, as he inches slowly.

My dear Lord, I love it when he says my name.

It's both a plea and permission.

Which I gladly give him.

As if a dam is breaking, we collide again. My arms wrap around his neck, and he once again pulls me closer. His hand finds my waist, then creeps beneath my shirt, the warmth of his hand now a scorching brand against my waist. He tugs me closer, his other hand, possessive and strong, snaking around my neck. Cal is kissing me as if he is a man starved. A man who has dreamed about this.

Thirsting for it.

Wanting it.

Like a man who is in love.

This one thought forces me to break our connection. We rest our foreheads together, catching our breath in the silent stillness.

Cal starts to chuckle. "I warned you."

My chest heaves trying to process what in the heck that was. "See?" I manage through shallow breaths. "Told you it would work."

As we sit unmoving (well, he sits), not wanting to break apart, something stirs within me. A desire. A desire to know what he meant when I overheard him talking to Denny in his office.

"Cal, I need to ask you something."

Our foreheads break apart, and he runs his hand down my hair, twisting the end strand. "I'll tell you anything."

"When you were on the phone with Denny earlier, what did you mean when you said that it took you months to get over something? What were you talking about?"

He chortles in disbelief as he teases me, tickling my side. "I knew you were eavesdropping."

A small giggle ripples through me. God, I love this playful version of Cal. "The walls are like tissue paper in that place. That's not my fault."

His laugh is short, but the sound fades as his expression shifts, growing serious. "Do you really want to know?"

"Yes."

"It will change everything." His palm trails up my arm and rests on my bare collarbone.

I know it will. And I don't give a crap. If he is about to say what I suspect he is, then nothing will ever be the same. A man only kisses a woman like that if it means ...

"It took me months to get over *you*. Because when we worked together"—he sighs, then locks eyes with me—"I fell in love with you."

Yep, there it is.

But I still have questions. "That night, though, when we went out for drinks, and we almost kissed, you—"

"Stopped it." His mouth twitches. "Worst mistake of my whole life. I should have claimed you right then and there."

"But why? Why did you stop it?" I ask as I trace his eyebrow with my thumb. His eyes slide shut at the contact.

"I was trying to be professional. Plus," he pauses, "I heard about Niko."

"But I wasn't dating Niko then. We were only talking."

"I didn't know how serious things were," he explains quietly. "I saw a few of the texts, yeah, but I didn't want to interfere."

"Wait. You saw some of my texts? Cal ..." I draw his name out in exasperation and pull back slightly. This is a huge invasion of privacy.

"I know! I know! I'm sorry. You left your phone out and yes, I looked. I'm not proud of it, and it's something that won't happen again, I can promise you that. I was just drunk on jealousy, which isn't an excuse. But it is the truth."

I chew on my bottom lip, stalling. thinking. Deciding. I mean, I would be lying if I said that I haven't done some pretty shady stuff in the name of love. And jealousy.

Probably both.

Am I willing to let whatever this is, slip through my fingers? And for what? A lapse in judgement?

No. No, I'm not.

I meet his eyes and he looks like he wants to vomit. He's probably saying a silent prayer hoping he didn't just ruin this before it even started.

I slap him on the chest, playfully. "You're lucky I like you."

The breath he lets out sounds like it's been locked inside him for days. "Oh, thank God."

He leans in and kisses me. It's soft, careful, and apologetic, like he's testing the ground after an earthquake.

"I'm sorry," he murmurs against my lips.

I pull back just enough to grin. "You're forgiven."

His brows lift. A slow, sly smile breaks through. "Wait. You *like* me?"

"Don't get carried away," I tease. "Only a little."

He laughs, shaking his head, eyes still searching mine.

"You can continue," I add, folding my arms like I'm giving him the floor—because I am.

And he does. "Like I was saying, you deserved to find out for yourself if Niko was what you wanted—without me making it harder."

"So you were trying to be a gentleman."

He nods.

"But don't you see? You took away my right to make that decision for myself. Because, Cal ..." Now it's my turn to confess. "I wanted to keep kissing you that night. My choice would have been you. Yes, I was talking to Niko. But when we were together, and only working, I felt so safe. So comfor—"

The confession stops; my mind whirls with more questions. "But why push me away the weeks after, and start arguments with me? I thought I had done something wrong that night. If anything, you propelled me to Niko. He showed up that night, right after you left."

He exhales slowly. "I didn't know that." His hands find my back, firm and deliberate, tugging me closer to him. "I'll say it again," he murmurs low, "worst mistake of my life."

Our breathing quickens, matching heartbeats. *Please kiss me again.*

He doesn't. Instead, he continues to explain as his words brush against my skin. "I pushed you away because being near you—being around you—was unbearable. It still is. Not being able to touch you, kiss you, or run my fingers through your hair…" He breaks slightly. "It's its own kind of hell."

His Adam's apple rolls as he swallows hard before he continues. My attention stays on him. "But over time, as we worked together, I learned to love what I could get when I was with you. My heart beating faster when our shoulders would brush, your sharp retorts at me when we would bicker." I chuckle.

He pauses, the silence stretching as he gathers his thoughts. "A few months after you were done shadowing me, I finally realized how badly I'd messed up," he says quietly. "I decided to call you. But Niko answered." His jaw tightens. "He told me you were in the shower."

My heart stops beating. "Y-you called me?" he nobs. "Niko never told me about that phone call."

"Are you surprised?"

"What? That you called or that he didn't tell me?"

Cal shrugs. "Both, I guess."

I snuggle in closer to him. "No, I'm not surprised he didn't tell me. Yes, I'm *shocked* you called." He smiles. "I really wish I would have answered the phone."

He drifts away, brow furrowing as the memory drags him back. "Right then, I knew I'd lost you. I had already lost myself when we were together."

"Are you still lost?"

His fingertips dig into my flesh. "I'm just waiting for you to find me."

I reach for him, my palms cupping his face, the manly scrape of stubble rough against my skin. "Hey," I whisper, forcing his attention on me. He locks his gaze with mine. "I found you. In your office, at this hotel, in the room, then the storage closet, at the ball. And now here. I'll always find you. Please don't lose me again."

He pecks my lips. "I won't."

I smile. "Good. Now that's out of the way, I do have one more question."

He laughs. "My girl is so curious."

"When it comes to you, yes, I am."

"Sure. You can ask in a second." His hand cups my head, and he pulls my lips to his, kissing me again. Warmth spreads through me, soft and steady, until all I can feel is him. His closeness, his calm, the quiet promise hidden in the way he holds me.

It's all so perfect.

He pulls back. "Okay, now you can ask."

Not sure how I'm going to talk because there's no air left in my lungs. *Lord, can this man kiss.*

Wait. What did I want? Oh yeah, a question. I pull in a breath. "What about the picture frame on your desk that you threw into the drawer? I got the impression you didn't want me to see it."

"I knew you were going to ask me that." He grimaces through a chuckle. "That was a picture of us. Remember, Denny took it the first week. Before—"

"—before you pushed me away and treated me like crap." I wince at my accusation. He chuckles, unfazed, then runs his hand up my arm slowly. Deliberately. I stop breathing. "Why did you keep it?" I implore, the curiosity killing me.

For an entire year, that picture sat on his desk. He didn't forget me. Us.

He tilts his head, and our eyes meet. "I wanted to remember you. Every day, I would look at it and start my day with you. I tried to move on and date other people, but then I would come into work, and there you would be. On slow days, I would sit and stare at it, curious about what you were doing. Who you were kissing. Wondering if it was still Niko. Hoping you were happy." He pauses and swallows. "I know it wasn't healthy and just a picture, but I wanted more, and if that was all I could ever get, well …"

His words trail off. Then, a faint crease forms on his brow, uncertainty dashing into those steady green eyes. "Do you still want him? Niko," he asks, raw and vulnerable. His fingers find my back again and tighten, bracing for my answer.

"I'm not kissing him right now, am I?" I quip back as I inch closer, silently begging him to take my mouth again.

A low laugh slips out, and he leans away enough to separate us. "No," he admits. "You're not. But you still haven't answered my question, Rose." He pauses. "And I need an answer."

Yesterday, I might have hesitated. There was a time I would've let Niko weave his way back into my life, convincing myself there was still something left to salvage. But not now. Not after today.

Not after Cal's steady presence.

His careful touch.

Or knowing stares.

Not after holding him.

And definitely not after that kiss.

Cal is my future.

"No, I don't want him." I've never been so certain of anything.

I soak him in, the spark of his skin chasing away any lingering thought of Niko. "There's only you. Cal. Only. You."

His chest rises and falls, the uncertainty leaving him in a quiet rush of relief and exhaustion. "You bring me to my knees, Rose Sheridan. And I hope I never stand again."

Then he pauses. "The storm we breathe."

I chuckle. "What?" A memory floods my head. "Wait, the neon sign in your office above the door." He nods. "Why are you saying that now?"

His arms encase me. "It's there to remind me of what I've endured to get to where I am in life. And how I've made it out on the other side. Sometimes you need to experience the storms of life, and breathe them in, in order to make it out alive."

He holds my gaze as he speaks, his voice steady. It slides under my skin and stays there. "People can be our storms too," he says softly. "But the good kind. The ones that shake us, challenge us. Love isn't about avoiding conflict, Rose. It's about choosing to stay—right in the middle of it—together. You face the chaos, breathe it in, and find strength in it."

Something inside me cracks open.

We connect.

We ache.

We breathe.

His words settle between us, warm and grounding. "You're my storm, Rose," he whispers. "Things are rough now, but we'll stand together. We'll find our calm inside the chaos."

My hands lift to his face, my thumbs brushing the line of his jaw. "And you're mine."

Our lips collide. It's a rush that feels inevitable, wild, and right. The world falls away, leaving only the thunder of our hearts and the storm we've chosen to survive together.

Chapter Thirteen
11:23 p.m.

Cal

T he world disappears.

Rose tastes like every regret I've ever had and every moment I've ever wanted. She presses into me, fingers curling in my shirt, and I lose myself in her, in the warmth, in the hunger I've kept buried for far too long.

I want to be stuck in this elevator forever. Because I can't believe after all this time, I have Rose Sheridan in my arms. Her lips on mine. Every kiss, every touch of her hand, is a promise. Of what, I don't know.

But a promise.

Finally, it's all out in the open. Our feelings, the past, what we want from each other … all of it.

We make out like teenagers. No idea for how long. Time has stopped with each pass of her lips. And as I grab her hips and tug her to me, my phone buzzes, loud in the quiet, shattering the moment.

With a growl, we break apart, both of us breathing hard. I curse under my breath, yanking the phone from the floor beside us.

It's Denny.

"Of course," I mutter, hanging my head in defeat.

The man has always had impeccable timing. Why am I surprised that he would call right at this very moment?

"Who is it?" Rose asks, her cheeks flushed, lips swollen, and out of breath.

"Denny."

"Answer it. It could be a lead about my mom." She skims her fingers under my collar. "Once this is all over, we will continue this."

I trail my hand down her curls, running my thumb along her cheek before grazing her neck. My mouth follows the path, and I finally arrive at her exposed shoulder, peppering it with kisses as my phone continues to blare beside me. "Promise?" I whisper, praying she wants the same.

With a grin, she gently kisses my lips. "Promise."

God, this woman is going to be the death of me. I love it.

I swipe to answer. "Cal."

His voice is brisk, no small talk. "What in the heck took you so long to answer? Where are you?"

"Trapped in an elevator. The lights went out at the hotel."

"You're kidding? Where's Rose?"

Straddling my lap. But I don't say it. Her grin mirrors mine as the taste of her lingers. Her waist is in my grasp, and I squeeze as she rolls off of me. "She's right here."

There's a pause. "Stuck in the elevator with you?"

"Yes."

Another pause. "Are you smiling?"

"I am."

He heaves out a breath. "Forget I asked."

I look over at Rose, who is now leaning against the elevator wall. *Oh my God*, she mouths while she buries her face in her hands. I have to laugh. "What's up, Denny?" I ask, hitting the speaker. "The reception won't be great in here, so be quick. I might lose you."

"Diane mentioning Maggie in the note is eating me alive. There has to be a reason. It's our only lead." He stops, almost as if he isn't sure he should continue. "So, I did some digging into Maggie's family."

My attention doesn't leave Rose as her eyes fly open in my direction. "Go on," I implore. "Rose is right here."

Denny's voice fills the small elevator. "Turns out Maggie's parents were hiding some pretty heavy stuff. They were running an identity theft scheme—credit cards, fake accounts, you name it. Pulling in serious money."

Rose stiffens beside me, her hand flying to her mouth. "What?"

"Rose, you didn't know?" Denny asks sharply.

"No, I didn't," she admits, my eyes on her. "How long had that been going on?"

Denny exhales. "From what I was able to dredge up, at least two years. Possibly more."

Rose chimes in again as something akin to realization flashes on her face. "As shocked as I am, this makes sense."

"How so?" Denny asks.

Rose and I glance at each other. "I think it's time to tell Denny what you told me earlier."

Denny hears this loud and clear. "You have to tell me anything that might help, Rose. Anything at all."

Rose bends over closer to the phone. "I was telling Cal earlier that growing up, Uncle Pete and Aunt Jenny always had money trouble. They resented my mom since she was more financially stable. Uncle Pete was the type who always hated people who had money. But then, before the fire, things changed."

"How did they change?" Denny's question is sharp, and I know from experience that it signals note-taking time. I can almost hear the insistent scratching of the pen on the paper.

"Suddenly they got a new car and did a complete renovation of their house. Maggie's birthday party that year was massive. And Aunt

Jenny started dressing better. Uncle Pete bought her a huge diamond ring. Little things like that. As a kid, you don't make much of it, but as an adult, when I thought back on it, it seemed odd. Especially since they weren't working. When it was happening, Mom would always comment that she thought maybe they had won the lottery." Rose snickers at the last part. "It honestly seemed to be the only real explanation. But after the fire, Mom never talked about it again."

"Do you know if your mom ever asked them about it? Before the fire, I mean," he inquires.

She shrugs as if Denny can see her. "We were so young at the time. Maggie was excited about the changes, and of course, I thought the new car was awesome. But I was twelve, Denny. My friends were my world. I was wearing preteen/kid goggles. I didn't give the adults a second thought."

"Hmmm…" Denny hums into the phone.

"What are you thinking, Denny?" I scoot against the elevator wall alongside Rose and rest the phone on my leg. Our shoulders brush, and her hand finds my thigh. A sign that what we just did wasn't a onetime thing.

"I had some suspicions, so I sat down and really dug my heels into the case file, which I should have done months ago."

"What did you find?" I ask.

"Rose, I read your mom's statement about the fire. We know she was there that night, and according to her, she figured it out and went to confront them."

"Why wouldn't she have just gone to the police?" I ask.

"My guess is she wanted to protect Maggie." He pauses. "Anyway, there's a chance that fire wasn't …" Static cuts in.

I glance at Rose. She's chewing on her nails, processing everything.

"Denny, you're breaking up."

"Can …y … hear me?" he asks through the now unsteady call.

"Barely," I reply, picking up my phone. As if that will help with the connection.

"I … think … mom …" Then the line goes dead.

The words hang unspoken and heavy. Rose's face crumples, disbelief written in every line.

"You think my mom … confronted them?" Her question shakes as she turns to me.

I reach out, gripping her hand tight. "Hey. We don't know yet. But it's a real possibility. First the note, and now we find out this? It makes me wonder if maybe Maggie found out what was going on? Maybe she discovered your mom knew?" I rest my head on the elevator rail and sigh as questions swirl and dance. I turn and stare at Rose's profile; her perfectly sloped nose and long eyelashes taunt me. "Why else would your mom write that?"

Rose offers a slight nod before her eyes meet mine. "I don't know. But if Denny's right …"

I swallow hard. "Then we need to call Maggie. Now."

Chapter Fourteen
The night of the fire

Diane

I didn't want to believe it.

Pete is my baby brother. My family.

I stare down at the envelope in my hand, disbelief twisting in my gut. He wouldn't sink this low—or at least, I never thought he would. And yet here I am, standing on his doorstep, ready to face him and his wife.

We weren't especially close growing up, but there was always fierce loyalty. Back then, life was simple. We had parents who loved us and a home that felt safe. But somewhere along the way, he changed. We both did. I threw myself into school, earned my PhD in theoretical physics, built a career from the ground up. And all while getting married, becoming a mother, and then losing the man I loved. It wasn't easy. But my work became my lifeline, the thing that held everything else together.

That is when the resentment set in for my brother.

He was always terrible with money. And lazier than he'd ever admit. One bad business venture after another, half-baked investments, pyramid schemes. All of them left another dent in his bank account. And his pride. Eventually, it all caught up with him, and it was impossible to make ends meet.

But lately ... things have been different. Too different. New cars in the driveway. Designer clothes. A freshly remodeled house. I've wondered where the money came from, but I minded my own business.

He seemed to have turned things around, and I let myself believe it. Maybe one of his wild schemes finally worked. Maybe, for once, luck was on his side. And honestly, I was glad for all of them.

Especially for Maggie. That little ball of sunshine has always felt like my own. Watching her smile made it easy to ignore the doubts whispering in the back of my mind.

Rose and Maggie are inseparable and thick as thieves. They grew up side by side, and even though they're cousins, it is also a friendship. One that started with scraped knees and shared secrets. From playground swings to school plays. They built a world that belonged only to them. They know each other's moods like weather patterns.

And as they grow and approach their teen years soon, that closeness isn't fading. It's only growing and becoming quieter and deeper. Like a hurricane that builds and builds surrounded by warm waters. Pete, Jenny, and I are those warm waters. Supporting them and loving them through it all.

The future felt so bright. All of us working together to raise these young ladies.

Until Pete accidentally sent me an email.

It was a lazy Sunday afternoon. Rose was reading alone in her room, and I was catching up on some work emails. As I was busy deleting unnecessary fluff from my inbox, I got a ding. It was from Pete, and the subject line read, *Let me know what you think.* Curiosity got the best of me, and of course, I opened it, thinking it was for me.

I couldn't have been more wrong.

Turns out, it was supposed to go to one of his so-called "friends," but it landed in my inbox instead. An honest error since my personal email starts with my dead husband's first name. The same name this mystery man has.

Tom.

At first, I thought nothing of it. The sparse email contained only two phrases: "See attachment," followed by "and we will talk." All of it seemed innocent enough. Until I opened the attachment, and my eyes bugged out of my head. My brother was emailing this Tom in order to lure him into the twisted life of identity theft he created. And of course my brother would get a cut of whatever money Tom made.

And who knows how many other people he has enticed?

Included in the email were bank statements under different names. Credit applications with stolen Social Security numbers. Hundreds of them. Death certificates of small children.

I was staring, trying to process it all. My hands were shaking as the realization hit me. I wanted to believe there was some explanation. That maybe this was something innocent. But there wasn't. There couldn't be.

Within minutes, everything became clear.

The sudden windfall.

The new cars.

The remodel.

Jenny's new clothes and jewels.

It all made so much sense.

I let the email sit for a few days, trying to decide what to do. Several times a day, I would examine the email again, attempting to find an alternative explanation. Anything that wouldn't paint my brother as a monster.

But it wasn't there.

After reading the email, for a millisecond, I contemplated looking the other way.

But I couldn't. How many lives were destroyed because of his greed? How many life savings did he steal? People's futures and livelihoods. Gone.

Now here I am, standing on their front porch, ready to show them what I found.

I've decided to give him a chance to explain himself. Maybe if he knows I know, we can work together to make it right.

I inhale deeply, steeling my resolve, and knock on the door.

Immediately, it swings open, and I'm met with my sister-in-law's toothy smile and the smell of cinnamon. "Diane! Hi! This is a surprise! Come in!" Jenny has always been the most energetic person in any room. Maggie is just like her. But today, knowing what I know, that excitement is annoying me.

"Hey, Jenny." With a heavy heart full of dread, I step into their spotless living room. The faint scent of cinnamon comes from a small candle that rests on the fireplace mantel. A fireplace that wasn't there a few years ago. The flame ripples, mirroring the sharpness in my chest.

Clutching the folder of documents, I survey the newly remodeled house, now through fresh eyes. Fresh paint and framed artwork adorn the walls. New furniture rests on a soft plush carpet. I glance over the now open-concept space to the kitchen. They had to demolish a wall to achieve that.

It's as if a Home Depot exploded everywhere. New granite counter-tops, cabinets, appliances, a dining room table and chairs. All of it. The whole house is a perfectly curated photographed spread in *Better Homes and Gardens* magazine from an article titled "How to Get Your Dream Home." Because that's what they got. Their dream.

But at other's expense.

A question plays on repeat. What will happen to Pete and Jenny once this all comes out? I'm sure they will be arrested. Then a trial followed by jail time, more than likely. *What will this do to Maggie?*

"The house looks great." I deadpan as the compliment is flat and tastes bitter on my tongue. My brother emerges from the back hallway. "Hey, sis! What brings you by?" His smile, familiar and bright, greets me. He shoves his hands into his pants pockets.

Seeing him here now, happy and content for the first time in a long time, is going to make what I have to do that much harder.

I square my shoulders and jut out my chin. "We need to talk." The four words come out sharp, and the courage I had driving over here is waning after seeing him.

He picks up on my tone, and his expression tightens. He knows me too well. Growing up together will do that. "What's this about?"

"Look, Pete, you know how much I love you guys and Maggie"—I force out a grin—"and that there's nothing I wouldn't do for you three."

His eyebrows scrunch together. "You're acting weird. What's going on, Diane?" Jenny joins her husband's side, equally nervous and unsure. Coming over here like this is strange. We have never been a swing-by-just-because type of family.

Here goes nothing.

"You tell me," I say, dropping the folder on the coffee table. Papers spill out—printouts, screenshots, bank statements, names. "Because it looks like you've been stealing people's identities."

Both of them watch the envelope sail through the air. Jenny gasps as soon as she sees what it contains. Her face pales. Pete curses under his breath while rubbing the back of his neck. "How did you find out?"

"You might want to double-check who you send emails to. Tom7 612@gmail.com. I'm pretty sure this"—I wave my hand over the mess of papers—"wasn't meant for my eyes, was it?"

He's eerily quiet as he bends down and picks up one of the random copies of a social security card and studies it. Minutes pass, and the silence lingers longer than I'm comfortable with. My brother has always been a talker. So much so that he would get on my nerves. But now? This is the quietest I have ever seen him. In my life.

I forge ahead. "I couldn't ignore it." I'm shaking, but I don't stop. He continues to weed through the papers. "All that money—new cars, this house—it was so odd because it came out of nowhere. I wondered how or what, but it was none of my business. This though?" I jab my finger in the direction of the envelope. "This is fraud. It's wrong, and you both know it."

A sob comes from where Jenny stands next to Pete as she grabs onto his arm. Pete drops the papers he was holding, his face hardening. "You don't know what you're talking about."

"I know enough," I fire back. "That email you sent me by mistake. It had everything. What I printed is only a fraction of what it contained."

Jenny shifts into him, whispering something I can't make out. He shakes his head as her hands tremble, resting on his forearm.

You can hear a pin drop in this newly remodeled living room. The silence stretches on; our breathing is the only melody to this madness. None of us moves. Jenny is the first to break the tension. Pleading. "Diane, please. You don't understand. We didn't mean for it to get this far. All we wanted was not to struggle anymore. We were so sick of always wondering where the next paycheck was coming from. Or how we were going to give Maggie basic school supplies." She turns away, clearly exasperated. "You wouldn't understand," she mumbles under her breath.

I'm used to this kind of biting comments from these two. And I refuse to feel bad about working hard. Granted, more than half of the money I have comes from my late husband's estate. But the other half is from good old-fashioned hard work and dedication.

So many times, I offered to help them out financially. Only for them to refuse and throw some kind of snide remark my way. And I'm over it. They have crossed a line this time. Getting involved with an MLM is one thing. But this??

"It doesn't matter what you meant," I bite out, heat rising. "It matters what you've done."

Pete stares, pointed. "What do you plan to do with all of this?"

"I *should* go to the police," I state firmly but then sigh. "But the last thing I want is for Maggie to lose her parents. So, I came here to offer help. I won't say anything about what I found out if you put a stop to this right now. No questions asked."

Pete slams his hand against the wall. "NO!" I flinch.

I'm stunned at his outburst, but also his refusal to consider that what he is doing is immoral is something I can't get past. Is he so blinded by greed? "No?" Shock courses through me at his stubbornness.

"You heard me." He closes the distance slowly, each step deliberate. Cold eyes rip into me. Unblinking. Like he's already decided the ending to this little argument. "And now, you're not going anywhere," he hisses.

An amused chuckle leaves my lips. "*I'm not going anywhere?*" Mockingly, I throw his words back at him. "Are you serious, Pete? You can't keep me here. You sound like a crazy person."

I take a second and really study this man. My brother. The only other person on the planet who remembers my parents when they were young and our grandparents before they passed. The one who would secretly flush my mom's gross beef stew down the toilet for me so that I didn't have to sit at the table all night. My brother, who covered for me when I snuck out to meet my boyfriend when I was fifteen.

Somewhere along the way, life's hardened him. He's different. I've known that for a while now, and maybe I was too afraid to notice. But at this moment, I see him. I really see him. And I don't like the dishonest and scary person staring back at me.

My only sibling and I stand off in this house. A house paid for with tainted money and greed. I refuse to be here for another second. I'm done. Frantically, I bend to pick up the papers.

Jenny finally speaks up. "Let her go, honey." Reaching for each paper, I keep my eyes glued to the table.

She sounds so sad. And defeated.

Who knows? Maybe she's done living this lie. It can't be easy. The deceit. But her feelings are the least of my worries right now. I've gotta get out of here and decide on my next move.

In a split second, my brother yanks my arm, hard. His masculine grip tightens like nothing I've ever experienced as his fingers dig into my flesh. "Diane, stop! Let's sit down and talk about this."

Oh, now he wants to talk after he threatened to keep me here. *Yeah, okay. Not happening.*

Twisting my arm, I attempt to get out of his grasp, but his grip only tightens. His meaty fingers dig in more, the pressure sharp and painful.

"Let me go!" I snap, full of both fear and anger.

He doesn't.

The tension snaps. It's electric with panic. He pins me with a look; his jaw hardens as my first, clumsy tug at his grip does nothing. I yank back again, but his hold only tightens. Fear heats my palms.

Desperate, I drag my nails across his skin. Sharp and frantic. Anything to make him loosen his fingers so I can get the heck out of this house.

Crimson red streaks appear on his forearm. He stumbles back and yelps, freeing me while jerking his arm away.

And knocking the candle over in the process. It wobbles and then topples off the mantle. Wax splatters, and in an instant, the flame catches on the edge of the curtain.

The scent of cinnamon thickens as Jenny screams. My pulse spikes, and horror roots me to the spot for half a second before I see it. Flames racing across the room, faster than anything I've ever seen. My stomach drops.

"Get water!" I shout, snatching up a throw blanket and beating at the fire, but it's useless. All I did was make it worse. The flames leap wildly, devouring the drapes in seconds, turning them to ash before crawling across the floor, hungry for more.

"Jenny, where is the extinguisher?!" Pete screams while opening the hall closest. They scramble, searching.

Abandoning the blanket, and passing Pete and Jenny, I run to the kitchen. Desperation fills me as I open a cabinet and find a bucket. I throw it under the faucet and turn it on.

This is taking too long! I glance back, and the flames and the walls are engulfed, glowing orange and red as the fire eats everything it touches.

Panic surges inside me as smoke fills the space. Fast. My throat tightens, and the cough that erupts out of me is uncontrollable. Frantically, through the smoke, I search for my brother and sister-in-law. Nothing we do is going to help. There's only one thing we can do. "We have to get out!" I yell over the crackling, popping and hissing from the inferno.

Pete sprints to the kitchen and whips open a drawer, yanking out a box, an envelope, and a money bag maybe. I don't know.

Out of my periphery, Jenny dashes to the mudroom, grabbing a bag from a hook to help. Pete shoves everything inside. *I guess they didn't find the extinguisher.* "I can't leave this!" Sheer panic and despair paint his features. And Jenny is right by his side.

Is this what he has become? His house is going up in flames fast, and possessions are the only thing he's thinking about. Not his wife. Not his sister. But stuff.

"Forget it! Leave it!" I yank Jenny's wrist. "We have to move!"

But she jerks away and sprints back to the living room. To the fire. With her arm up, she covers her mouth and coughs through the smoke. She reaches for something on the mantel. A vase, followed by some more breakables. "Give me a minute!" she screams through a strangled cough.

The fire roars, loud and relentless. A hungry beast swallowing everything. Thick black smoke surrounds us, increasing with each passing second. My lungs burn, and it's getting so much harder to breathe. Terror and panic crash over me, flooding my chest. The heat from the flames is becoming too much.

It *is* too much.

I try one last time.

I beg.

I plea.

"Come on! Please!" Tears sting my eyes. Not just from the smoke, but from fear. And sadness.

My brother's scream cuts through the black smoke and flames. "Jenny, run upstairs and empty the safe!" he commands. "Get the cash, and I'll grab the file box. We can't leave that behind. Hurry!" He's charging up the steps now, dragging the bag weighed down with more things they have added. Jenny is sobbing, too far gone to listen to my pleas as she follows Pete to the second floor and they disappear from view.

I stumble back, choking as my vision blurs. The heat is unbearable. The entire room is the glow of fire spreading fast, devouring everything.

Covering my mouth with my shirt, I crouch down on all fours and attempt to get my bearings. Surveying the surroundings, I realize my sole means of escape is the back porch sliding door. The pathway there is narrow. And if I go now, I can make it. The flames and smoke engulfing the first floor will consume me if I wait another second.

Rose's face fills my mind, and pure adrenaline pushes me forward. *I am not going to die in this house. I am not leaving my daughter!*

Determination propels me as I crawl to my only means of escape. I reach and grab the handle. Heat sizzles my flesh as I cry out, flipping my hand from the pain. Without any time to think, I whip off my shirt and wrap it around my hand. "I'm sorry," I apologize, knowing Pete and Jenny won't hear me. "I'm so, so sorry." Regret seeps into me, thick and suffocating like the smoke, leaving no room to breathe.

If I hadn't come over, this would have never happened.

Now, in only my bra and jeans, I slide open the door and burst outside. Instantly, fresh air fills my lungs. A coughing fit follows, and I sprint to the backyard, then collapse onto the cool grass. But I don't stay on the ground long. I leap up, throw my shirt back on, and make a beeline for the neighbor's next door. I find them already on the front lawn, mouths gaping open as thick black smoke pours out of the home. "Call 911!" I scream.

The woman hands me her phone. "Here. They are already on the line."

I yank the phone from her and immediately start barking commands to the dispatcher. "Hurry! You have to send help! My brother and his wife are inside. The whole house is burning!" I'm coughing like crazy, and it's hard to breathe. Then the dizziness starts. Everything blurs and spins around me. Chaos envelopes the entire neighborhood. The dispatcher says something, but I don't hear her. "What?!" I yell into the phone.

Her reply doesn't register because the last thing I hear is the crack of timber and Jenny's scream that follows.

Glass shatters as the entire house erupts in a ball of flames.

The phone falls from my grasp and sinks into the lawn. The world narrows to heat and smoke as I drop to my knees.

Watching it burn.

Chapter Fifteen
Three days prior
The night of the kidnapping

Diane

Fingers snap in my face, sharp and impatient, pulling me back to reality.

At least, I think that's what that is.

"Wakey wakey." A voice cuts through the snapping.

My chin drops as pain drums through my skull, each throb sharp and merciless. When I lift my head and force my eyes open, the world swims. Blurry angles, cookie-cutter pictures hang on the surrounding walls, with a single lamp burning too brightly. A round table sits to my right.

Is this a … a hotel room? Am I still at the Black Onyx?

I try to raise my hands, but they won't move. A zip tie bites into my wrists behind me, rough and unyielding, tethering me to the chair. My ankles are bound, too. I look at my injured foot, and the memory of the incident brings a searing pain that shoots up my leg. Panic spikes sharp and fast.

"What …" I swallow what feels like nails. "Where am I?"

"You're *finally* awake."

The voice comes from the corner. Almost gentle. But it doesn't soothe me.

It chills me.

The ringing in my ears makes it hard to hear clearly.

I squint through the haze. A figure stands across the room, shadowed, half-hidden by the dim light. Watching.

I look around the room again, and the decor becomes sharper, taking shape. All roaring 20s but still out of focus. "Is this a room at the Black Onyx?"

"You were always so smart." The sarcasm cuts through the biting reply.

"You hit me," I remember, my memory appearing in fragments.

The parking garage.

Footsteps behind me.

Pain exploding behind my skull.

Then nothing.

"You were making things ... difficult. Running and then hiding in the garage." The figure steps closer, but not enough for me to see clearly. A mask of shadows, which I'm sure is deliberate.

Fear claws through me, but anger sparks beneath it. "If it's money you want—"

A soft laugh cuts me off. Not cruel. Not kind. If anything, I hear confidence. "Maybe it's about the money, maybe not. But more importantly, it's about what people know. What they dig into when they shouldn't. And what they find out."

My pulse thunders as I squint my eyes shut, trying to soothe the pounding building in, coupled with confusion. "What are you talking about?"

"You always wanted answers, Diane. You always asked too many questions."

Hearing my name strikes me harder than the blow to my head.

Whoever this is—they know me.

And the voice. It's familiar, yet not.

All the grogginess is now gone as I straighten against the plastic ties, my breath catching. I study the figure more closely. "Who are you?"

They tilt their head, stepping close enough now that I can make out the faintest outline. The shape is so ... familiar.

But they stay barely out of the light.

"Someone who should have been your family," they say, low and steady. "And the daughter of someone you should have left alone."

My blood runs cold.

"*Maggie...*" The name trembles on my tongue, but I don't speak it. I can't. It's not possible. Because if I'm right, if it's really her, then everything I thought I knew about the girl I raised, about the girl my daughter loves like a sister, was a lie.

No. It can't be.

Whoever this is, creeps closer, and though their face is still partially hidden, the heat of their breath hits me when they speak. "You've made this harder."

The zip ties dig into my skin as I shift, trying to find some give. There's none. Though my throat feels like sandpaper, I keep my words from trembling. "Why are you doing this?"

The figure doesn't flinch. Doesn't move. "Because you couldn't stop digging. You had to know the truth. You couldn't leave us alone."

Ignoring the ache in my skull, I continue. "If this is about your ..." I stop myself, not wanting to give away that I might know who this is. "Do you think hurting me helps anything?"

She stays silent.

I clench my fists, fighting to keep my thoughts straight and temper in check. If this is truly Maggie, then I need to probe deeper.

The silence presses in on me as sweat beads on my hairline. Finally, the figure steps closer, their face still cloaked by the lamp's shadow. "You already knew too much. You asked the wrong questions, Diane."

What are they even saying? It's like they're speaking in riddles as we talk in circles.

"I don't understand a single word coming out of your mouth," I say, completely bewildered.

Clearly, it's important that I get some answers here, since they're offering none. This is an obvious mind game to them. But not to me. I want to know what happened, so I'm going to ask some questions. Which means I can't lead on that I've put two and two together, and that this could be Maggie. And gosh, I pray that my suspicions are wrong.

My pulse spikes. I think back to the garage, the echo of footsteps chasing me, the blur of motion before everything went dark. "Did you hit me?" I hiss out. Then louder: "Or was it someone else? Who took me from the garage?!"

That gets a reaction. A slight tilt as they folds their arms. But no answer.

"Tell me!" I push, anger burning through the fear. "Who are you?!"

A low chuckle. "No. Some things you don't get to know."

Frustration coils through my body, hot and tight. I force myself to breathe, to focus. "You don't have to do this. Whatever this is, whatever you think is going on. Kidnapping me. Holding me hostage."

The figure shifts, leaning against the wall now. Calm. Too calm. Completely silent.

I press some more. "Look, just let me go. I won't say a word. Nothing has happened."

"It already has," they hiss. *What does that mean?*

As I listen and try to process, I search the tone, the cadence, the almost-familiar rhythm of the voice, and terror grips me. Deep down, I already know.

I can't say her name. Not yet. If I'm wrong, I tip my hand. But if I'm right…

Then I've been betrayed by someone I let into my home. Someone I trusted with my daughter.

And I don't know which possibility is worse.

My back heaves against the chair, each breath harder to pull in than the last. I press. "If you're angry with me, fine. If you hate me, fine. But hurting me? That won't fix what you lost."

They shift unsteadily, as if the words land somewhere beneath their skin. A dart of movement—arms tightening around themselves, chin dipping.

It's time to find out if my suspicions are right because this is pure torture.

"Is this about the fire?"

Suddenly, Maggie's back goes ramrod straight.

I can't believe it.

"I've been curious about that night. For a while now," she starts. The sudden hardness is gone, and it's almost as if the Maggie of old has returned. "So I guess you could say that curiosity killed the cat because I decided to research that night on my own. And my, my, my ... wasn't I blown backward. To find out that dear ole Aunt Diane was there."

Vivid memories that I'll never escape flood back as I choke on the words. "I tried. You have to believe me. I tried so hard to get them out."

She saunters toward me tauntingly. "I got the police report with a little help from a friend of mine in tech. I read your sob story in the report. If you had just left them alone, everything would have been fine. We were happier. Richer. I had a massive birthday party, for crying out loud! But because of you ... poof. Gone." She stops briefly to compose herself. But she can't. "You were there, Diane. Why? Why didn't you save them?" Her accusations begin to thin and waver. She's trembling. "You should have left us alone!! Why did you have to meddle? My parents are dead because of you!"

She swipes away a tear, and the tough-girl act vanishes. Replaced now by someone who's full of grief and anger. Grief at her loss, and anger at me because she thinks I'm responsible. "Maggie—"

"Don't say my name!" she screams as she charges forward, finally stepping into the light. And confirming what I already know.

Maggie has kidnapped me.

And I barely recognize the ghost facing me. Disheveled clothes hang off her body with a wildness in her eyes. *My God ... what happened to you?* This isn't the bright, laughing girl who used to hug me every morning or fall asleep on my couch while watching TV. This is someone hardened who's twisted into something unthinkable.

A cold, bitter laugh catches. Maybe it's shock. Maybe it's anger. Maybe it's the only way to keep myself from breaking. "So," I say, letting the sarcasm drip because I refuse to show her fear, "I take it you didn't go to Italy."

No sooner has the question left my mouth, Maggie's open palm slaps my cheek. My head whips to the side.

She raises her chin, proud of herself. "I wasn't about to go on your pity trip. Poor Maggie. Let's send her to Italy as a replacement for her loss. No, thank you. Besides"—she waves her hand over the room—"I have more important things to attend to."

Nothing I'm saying or doing is working. God, this is such a mess. "I know losing your parents was hard. But you weren't there that night. You don't know everything. The fire started, and I tried to get them to leave. I did. But all they cared about was grabbing ... stuff. Meaningless possessions." She stares at me, and my heart breaks open, all my memories taking me back to that night. "I escaped," I choke out, "but part of me never left that house." A silence settles. "Do you really think your parents would be happy to see what you are doing right now?"

She hinges forward, her hands bracing on the arms of the chair. Her face inches from mine. "If you want someone to blame, look in the mirror," she growls out completely ignoring my question.

Pushing off, she sits down on the bed, casually examining her nails. "Now it's Rose's turn. To see what it's like to live without both of your parents," she snaps, sharper now, yet trembling at the edges.

Those words hang heavy, rawer than anything else she has said.

She.

Maggie.

The girl I'd raised.

My niece.

And the one holding me captive.

Three days have passed. Maybe more.

Time blurs together in this dim hotel room, where the lamp burns too bright and the shadows are heavier than night itself. My wrists ache from the ties, raw, bleeding, and tender, but at least I can still wiggle them.

My cut foot from the garage, however, isn't faring so well.

I'm pretty sure an infection has set in. It's red, swollen, and I'm freezing. Which means I have a fever.

I'm freed of my restraints only a few times a day. Maggie unties me so that I can use the restroom. She keeps a gun trained on me, watching me go pee, which is super humiliating. And then stays by my side while I eat, gun in hand.

Always making sure I don't make a run for it. Or fight back.

Not that I haven't thought about it. But then my mind always circles back to Rose. Maggie will kill me if I risk anything. And I can't do that to my daughter.

My head pounds from the lack of sleep and coffee, no doubt.

God, what I wouldn't give for a cup of coffee right now and my big, fluffy bed.

Since I woke up, there are things I've noticed now that I'm more lucid. Maggie leaves occasionally when she gets a phone call. There is an adjoining room, the entrance of which is behind me, so my view is blocked. She slips into it periodically. And I suspect sometimes she isn't alone. Then she returns. Meaner and moodier than before.

Currently, she left the room through the main door to get me something to eat. She's been gone for a while. Or maybe she hasn't. Time is no longer something I can measure, which leaves me with my thoughts and unanswered questions.

But one still plagues me. Because let's face it, I have a lot of time to think.

Why hasn't Maggie killed me yet?

And I've come up with only one answer.

She can't.

Deep down, she loves me. And she can't kill her family. She's still feeding me and giving me water. She also ties me to the bed at night so I can sleep. Which is better than trying to rest hunched over in this chair. Why would she do all of that if her intention was to harm, or God forbid, kill me?

Ripping me from my thoughts, the door opens, and she steps inside with a bag. Water, crackers, a protein bar. The usual. It never changes. Hunger twists deep inside.

I hate that I have to rely on her for my basic needs. It makes me sick.

She doesn't set the gun down right away. Her fingers tighten around it instead, knuckles whitening. "I shouldn't even give this to you." Her eyes burn with fury. "You really screwed up, Diane."

A sharp pulse of confusion flashes through me. "Stop with the riddles already, Maggie. What are you talking about?"

The gun slams against the desk. I flinch, my pulse jumping. She steps closer, leaning in until I can smell her breath. "You wrote a note to Rose. And you said my name."

For a split second, relief washes through me like light breaking through clouds. "Someone found it?" My words tumble out too fast. "Did Rose talk to you? How do you even know that?"

Her expression twists with frustration. "Because the police have it! They showed it to her. And now they're asking questions. About me!" She jabs a finger toward her chest. "You dragged me into this mess, Diane!"

My stomach sinks. "Oh, I'm pretty sure you did that all yourself. But me? I didn't know you were involved in this," I shout back, my voice cracking. "I didn't know who was chasing me! There were seconds to write something. I thought I was going to die, and I wanted Rose to know how sorry I am." My voice softens, breaking on her name. "Because I am, Maggie. I'm so sorry about that night. I would've done anything to take it back."

Her face flickers with anger, pain, and a touch of confusion before hardening again. But in that one brief second, I see it. The girl I once knew. The one who used to call me family.

"I should let you starve." She tosses the white plastic bag with red Thank You's all over it onto the desk. Using another weapon, a knife, she cuts the ties. Then, she points her gun. Her neat and deliberate movements echo in the quiet space. "Eat."

I rip open the protein bar and take a bite, swallowing hard. "Maggie..." I implore, not daring to say it louder.

Her eyes snap to me, sharp and deadly, as her grip tightens around the gun. The warning is clear: don't.

I try again, coaxing more. "You don't have to keep me here. Rose would forgive you if you—"

Her laugh cuts through, high and brittle. "Forgive me? You really think that's what this is about?" She paces again, her movements jerky before she stops dead in front of me. "You've always been so sure you know what's best."

A tight pain grips my heart. "I only ever wanted to protect her. *And* you. You are like a daughter to me, Maggie. You *have* to know that."

"Don't you get it? I'm done being your token daughter," she spits out, lip curling.

Something inside me snaps. Anger rises fast and hot, drowning out every other thought. I can't hold it in anymore. "I let you into my home! Into my family! And this is how you repay me? God, you are so selfish!"

The same fury that fills me is now coursing through her body. She stands still, but she's shaking, and completely falling apart. "And guess what, Aunt Diane. You're uninvited from my life." A small evil grin rises as she stands there. "And soon ... permanently." That sinister grin disappears. I wonder what was behind that smile.

Hours blur together. I've lost track of time completely. Maggie keeps darting in and out of the adjoining room, her movements sharp and restless. She's unraveling—more agitated now, pacing like a caged animal. She even forgot to tie me back to the chair after my last bathroom break.

Desperation clings to her every breath. Something's shifted. I can feel it in the air, heavy and wrong, but I can't tell what's changed ... only that it has.

That's when it happens. Her phone buzzes, screen lighting up with a familiar name.

Her phone isn't normally out in the open. It's with her at all times. Either in her hand or in her pocket. But she slipped and left it on the table. And now I can see who is calling.

Rose.

Maggie freezes. Slowly, she picks up the phone, her hand white-knuckled around it. Her eyes cut to me, wild, blazing. "Not. One. Word."

Fear hits me hard, knocking the breath from my lungs. *So, this is who's been calling Maggie?* It doesn't add up. Maggie is Rose's person, the one she always turns to, so some of those calls… they had to be from Rose.

But not all of them. Maggie couldn't have orchestrated all of this on her own. There's no way. Which means Rose isn't the only one she's been in contact with. I'm certain of it.

She steps closer, crouching as she spews her venom. "If you try to warn her—if you say *anything*—I swear to you, Diane, I'll kill you before you finish the sentence."

My breath hitches. Rose is a phone call away. And I can't reach her. Not without risking her life. And losing everything I hold dear.

Chapter Sixteen
11:35 p.m.

Maggie

"**I**f you try to warn her—if you say *anything*—I swear to you, Diane, I'll kill you before you finish the sentence." Diane's throat rolls while I stand and watch. A single tear tracks down her cheek. Good. I'm enjoying seeing her sad and defeated way too much.

The phone won't stop vibrating as I study the screen one last time, unease coiling tight inside of me.

Rose.

My perfect cousin and supposed best friend.

God, I hate her.

All I ever heard growing up was how perfect she was. And the praise came from all directions. Her mom, school teachers, family members. Hell, my own parents applauded her at every turn. It was constant.

Rose is so beautiful.

Rose is so smart.

Rose got the lead in the school play. Again!

Rose.

Rose.

ROSE!!

My face and body were the only things I ever had working for me. The boys always liked me better because I was easy. Tall, blonde, and within reach for when they wanted someone to make them feel good. And I always made sure I was available. Rose didn't play their games, but miraculously, she won anyway. They'd fall all over themselves to get closer to her.

She was blessed in life.

And her looks.

She was naturally beautiful, and things came easily to her. Whether it was her laugh, her eyes, her stupid curls. Didn't matter. Thinking about it now makes the old rage claw back. She had better grades, better hair, better everything. And the worst part? She didn't notice what it cost me to be the one left behind.

Because through it all … she had a mom.

Mine was dead.

Literally overnight, I had nothing. Just an orphan taken in out of pity by her rich aunt. At the time, I thought I'd hit the jackpot. My parents were gone, but Diane had money. A lot of it. And suddenly, so did I. Money, clothes, a huge house.

But then, Rose was always there.

Perfect, precious Rose. She had it all before I showed up. Diane's love, her attention, every ounce of affection I was starving for. I told myself it didn't bother me, that I could handle sharing. But I hated how easily she had everything I wanted handed to her without ever lifting a finger.

For a brief time before the fire, I had a small taste of that life. Prior to my parents' death, things were improving for us financially. The days of being poor were behind us. As a kid, it didn't matter. My birthday party that year was epic! I was the talk of the school the following Monday. Not Rose.

Me.

So you can imagine my surprise when I found out about my parents' crimes and what happened that night. And the fire.

The identity theft never bothered me. Why should it? Mom and Dad did what they had to do. They found a way to make life easier for us when the world refused to.

Good on them!

The people they stole from? They didn't need the money. They were all too rich, or dead, to notice. I admired them for having the nerve to take what everyone else was too afraid to reach for.

What bothered me was Diane. Her self-righteous meddling and her desire to swoop in and try to help. Like she always did. We didn't need her! But of course, she took my life from me and then expected me to be grateful when I went to live with her.

I don't think so.

Eventually, I got smarter and decided things should balance out. It was Rose's turn to understand complete parental loss, and to know what it's like when the person you love is ripped away. When I learned about Diane's conference, how it lined up with my trip, I knew it wasn't a coincidence. It was an opportunity. And like my parents, I seized the opportunity.

I know they would be so proud.

And now here I am. At first, everything was going perfectly. That was until I found out *Cal* was involved.

Of course, it had to be him.

I remember when she shadowed him last year. My God, she couldn't shut up about how brilliant he was, how capable, how hot, how *good*. She ruined her chance, like she does with every man she dates. But now he's back in the picture, and if he digs deep enough, he could tear everything apart.

On the phone, I tried everything I could to keep her away from him. I planted doubts about his honesty and loyalty. Anything to make her second-guess him. Of course, she didn't listen. He convinced her he could save Diane and be the guy of her dreams. And maybe that's what makes me hate him most.

The man's beautiful, I'll give him that, and that's the problem. Hell, I know I would have thrown myself at him. It's not the first time I would steal one of her boyfriends without her knowing. Now he's here, still glued to her side, still pretending to protect her. In the same freaking hotel and breathing the same air. Every time I think about it, my plan and the walls tighten around me. All of it daring me to lose control.

Shaking all doubt I have, I refocus on the call. For a split second, I consider ignoring it. I know she's with him right now. But she'll just keep calling, and I can't afford her getting suspicious. Diane watches me, her wrists red, bleeding, and chafed from the ties. She's judging me, like she always did.

I swipe to answer and attempt to keep myself steady. "Hey."

"Hey," Rose's greeting crackles through the speaker, light but strained. A small sob releases from Diane at the sound of her daughter's voice. I glare at her as a warning.

The connection is weak and distorted which makes me wonder where she is. "You're not going to believe this," her words strain slightly, "we're stuck in the elevator."

I blink, thrown for a second. "What?"

"With Cal," she adds quickly. "There was an outage or maybe a power surge, and now we're trapped."

"Oh." That name. Cal. I can almost see him—the man with a hero complex, her safety net, and savior. Funny how everything always falls into line for her.

It makes me sick. Sweet, prudish Rose now has two men pining for her. First Niko and now this Cal.

I force a smile, reminding myself who I'm pretending to be. The fake Maggie. The lights went out here but only briefly, but I can't mention that. I'm not at this hotel.

I'm in Italy

I'm in Italy.

I'm in Italy.

"You woke me up. What's up?" I ask through the crackle.

She laughs, a small nervous sound coming through the phone. "What? Maggie, the up-all-night party girl is sleeping." Annoyance ropes around my gut because of her laughter at my expense. "Are you having fun?"

Honestly, I should answer this in the adjoining room like I have with all the others. Instead, I pace the length of the bed, back and forth, each step heavier than the last. Diane tracks me, and I know she's reading too much into every move. "How many times are you going to call me today and ask me that?" I curse under my breath at how sharp and defensive that sounded. Not knowing what to do with myself, I survey the room and sit on the edge of the bed, gripping the comforter until the fabric bunches in my fist. "Sorry, Rosie Posie," I mutter, trying to smooth the crack in my tone. "I'm tired. That's all."

I should probably also apologize for hanging up on her earlier. Fake Maggie wouldn't do that. "And I'm sorry I hung up on you. Blame it on the jet lag."

There's silence for a beat or two. "It's okay. And you're right; that's not why I called."

I shift, my pulse picking up as my knee bobs uncontrollably. "Then why?"

"Denny called us, you know, the lead detective on Mom's case," she affirms and pauses, expecting me to agree. I don't. "Anyway, he found out some things about my mom's visit to your parents' house the night of the fire."

A shiver runs through me as my hand clasps the phone. As I turn, Diane's focus becomes intense, anticipating Rose's next revelation. She's close enough to me that I'm pretty sure she can faintly hear Rose through the call.

Rose keeps talking. "He said they were involved in some kind of identity theft scheme. That they were making a lot of money from it. Did you know anything about that?"

I swallow. "No," I say quickly, too quickly. "Of course not."

"Hmmm … are you sure? I mean, I've been thinking about it. Like how they suddenly had so much money, the new cars, the house, the trips—"

"Rose, stop," I snap way too quickly, betraying more than I want her to hear. "Don't talk about them like that."

She hesitates. "I … I'm not trying to upset you, I just—"

"Well, you *are* upsetting me." I push off the bed and pace again, the phone digging into my ear. The vice grip in my gut cinches tighter with each pass of the room.

She knows. *God, this Cal guy is ruining everything!* The anger inside me churns and bubbles. I'm a volcano, rumbling with the pressure and ready to explode.

"Maybe we should talk about this later. After you've rested," Rose says gently. "You sound … off."

Her concern makes me want to scream. Why does she always sound so *perfectly composed* and careful? She doesn't mean to sound better than I do, but she does.

She is.

Always has been.

Always will be.

My grip tightens around the phone until my hand shakes. "I'm fine. I just—I have to go." The words tumble out too fast.

"Maggie—"I can't hear the rest. Jabbing the screen and ending the call in a frantic panic, I hurl the phone onto the bed. It bounces, landing face-down. The silence in the room is suddenly too loud. My pulse is everywhere—my ears, my head, my fingertips. I can't make it stop.

Rubbing my temples, I can sense Diane's gaze again. She's quiet. Until she's not.

"She'll notice," she says softly. "Rose knows you too well. She'll hear it and figure out something is wrong."

That does it. I snap.

"Who cares!" I scream as I spin toward her, yanking a zip tie from the bag and rebinding her hands. "I hate her! You both act as if she's perfect. Sweet, innocent, unbreakable Rose. But she's not. She's nothing without me."

Diane flinches as my thoughts spill over and my mind is in overdrive.

I see her.

In my thoughts.

And my dreams.

I see Rose smiling.

Her *perfect* smile. The one that makes people love her instantly.

Then I hear her laugh. God, I hate her laugh.

And I see the way Niko and now Cal gawk at her.

The way he never looked at me.

The way no one does.

She takes everything.

Every bit of attention, every ounce of love that should've been mine.

And now, for once, she's going to lose.

And know what it's like to be me.

Chapter Seventeen
11:47 p.m.

Rose

The darkness of the elevator hums as the flashlight from Cal's phone illuminates brightly at his side. Light floods the room in a harsh white glare, bleaching the surrounding walls. The air in this box is thick and hot as the fine hairs stick to my neck.

With those two phone calls, the mood in this closed-in box becomes so heavy with despair that you could almost taste it. Cal's standing near the control panel with his hand braced against the wall and his jaw tight. I haven't moved from the floor, arms wrapped around my legs. He's been quiet since the call with Maggie ended.

We both have.

"Something's off," he finally says.

My pulse quickens. "What do you mean?" I ask, but I'm pretty sure we are both thinking the same thing. Something about Maggie doesn't sit right. It's not just that strange phone call. She's been … weird. Ever since I told her Mom was missing, it's like she's been holding back.

"There was no reaction," he mutters. "You told her we were stuck in here, and she didn't ask if you were okay. Not once."

I blink, frowning. "You're right."

Nothing makes sense right now. Because the person on the phone ... that wasn't my Maggie. The girl who held me upright when I got drunk at Derek O'Malley's grad party. The girl who helped me stuff my bra when I went on my first date. And helped me pass trig so that I could graduate.

My Maggie. My best friend. My cousin. My confidant.

He turns toward me, eyes sharp in the dim light as his fingers drum a rhythm on his thigh. "I mean, doesn't she know you're claustrophobic?"

Dread slices through me. "She does. She's known since we were kids."

He nods grimly. "Then why wasn't there any hint of worry in her voice? She should've been panicking for you. I mean, I barely know you, and all I wanted to do was"—he turns back to the control panel—"help you."

Biting my lip, I replay the call. Her flat tone, the quick way she hung up, the outburst. Maggie always worries about me. Always. But not this time.

No matter how hard I attempt to breathe, this pressure coiling around me won't pass. And the worst part? I know exactly why. Maggie's acting guarded.

Because she's hiding something from me. And admitting that to myself is like betraying everything I thought we had.

Cal runs a hand over his hair, the wheels turning as he attempts to figure all this out. "She knows something, Rose. I'm sure of it."

Tears press at the back of my eyes, choking my words. "You think she's what? Like involved?" I'm sure I didn't hear *that* right. And I get where he's coming from; she's not being truthful, that much I'm sure of. But to imply that she's involved with my mom's disappearance.

Impossible. "Cal, Maggie isn't involved with my mom vanishing. There has to be another explanation."

Hopefully, saying it out loud will make it true. Because if I'm being honest, the possibility slides into my mind quicker than I would like. And the thought makes me sick. Digging my palms against my knees, I attempt to steady the tremor that comes with not wanting to believe the sense Cal is making.

He says nothing right away, as he interlocks his fingers and rests them along the base of his neck. He peers at the ceiling, as if any answers to this absolute crap show lay there. I watch him, wanting more than anything to be inside his head right now to know what he's thinking.

Then, with determination coupled with desperation, he bolts and presses the emergency button again, his words firm and controlled when he speaks into the panel. "Hello? We're still stuck in here. We need maintenance now. Is anyone there?"

Static crackles back at us, and then a voice. We both jolt in surprise. "Yes, sir. We hear you. We were made aware of the situation and ask for your patience while we work on this. There are two of you in there correct?"

Cal exhales hard, the muscle in his jaw twitching. "Yes. My name is Detective Cal Masters, and I'm stuck in here with Rose Sheridan. We are currently working on a case, and you need to work your magic and get us out of here as quickly as possible. Now! Do I make myself clear?"

"Yes, sir. We are doing our best. We should have you out shortly." The line goes dead.

I stand slowly, brushing off my jeans. The elevator is unexpectedly small, but my eyes stay on him. The worry etched on his face, the frustration in his movements. It's all for me. And my mom. It pulls me toward him like gravity.

Plus, the urge to be near him floods through me. Swamped with doubt and fear, my mind is a relentless tide. I miss the security of him all around me. And I know this is a fleeting hot moment, yet the weight of him in my arms lingers. I know I want to have this again. Forever.

"Cal," I plead. "Come here."

He turns, and before he can say anything, I close the distance. My hand finds his chest, steady, sure. His heart thunders beneath my palm. "Rose—"

I wrap my arms around his waist, turning my gaze to meet his. The longing I saw earlier is still there, but it's accompanied by a flash of something else. Fear, worry, or maybe doubt. "You're *stuck* in here with me, huh?" I joke, trying to lift the mood. We need that right now.

He chuckles, pulling me closer. Our foreheads connect, and his breath skates along my face. "There is no one else in the world I would rather be stuck with." His promise stirs something in me.

I arch on my toes, angling my neck as my desire lands on his lips. "Please," I beg softly. "Before we leave this box and my world falls apart again." Because right now, it's only us. As soon as those doors open, my mom is gone, Maggie's weird behavior looms large, and the storm continues to rage outside. For a few more minutes, I want it just to be us again.

As his gaze sweeps over my face, his eyes darken, the war raging inside of him written all over his features. Torn between reason and something deeper. The crease in his brow sends my heart plummeting.

Without warning, I'm catapulted back to the sidewalk outside a restaurant a year ago, waiting for a kiss that never came. That same feeling of rejection I felt that night floods my whole body once again.

He exhales, stepping back slightly, uncoiling my arms from his waist. With gentle pressure, he holds on to both of my wrists. "We can't. Not right now."

The words hit harder than they should. I deflate. "Because of the case," I say flatly.

"Yes, staying focused is really important, Rose."

I nod, pretending that doesn't sting. "Sure, focused."

Was that kiss, which happened barely minutes ago, a strategy? A way to steady me, to get me to trust him? Suddenly, Maggie's words come flooding back: *Please be careful. Something seems off about him. Then add in how he treated you the last time. I don't know … just some food for thought.*

But that's not what my gut is telling me.

Cal is trustworthy; I know it. Maybe it should've felt like he was using me to get in his good graces. But it didn't. There'd been something underneath it, something real. The memory still burns on my lips. The warmth of his touch, tender yet possessive, hums beneath my skin. It couldn't have been meaningless. It wasn't a fleeting moment.

His face softens, breaking me from my internal musings. "It's not rejection, Rose. This isn't like last year."

"Are you sure?" I ask as a war of doubt and hope swirls around me.

He lets go of my wrists and cups both of my cheeks. "As soon as this is all over, I promise to kiss you in the way that you deserve. When we aren't trapped and scared." His plump lips hover over my ear, his hot breath tickling my skin as he whispers. "And in a way you will always remember."

Well, okay then.

"I don't think I'll forget that last one," I confess.

He traces the curve of my neck with his fingertips. His lips follow, peppering sweet kisses on my skin. "I don't want to lose this," he promises, meeting my eyes. "You and me, Rose … I'm not going anywhere. I'm done running away. Hell, I think I've been running *toward* you all along."

As I listen to his words, the promise within them wraps around me like a soft blanket. Words that are impossible to forget.

So I make one of my own.

With the slightest graze, I run my nose over his. "We won't lose this."

The green in his eyes comes alive with our promises. Because that is exactly what I want.

Silence hangs charged with a future we are both envisioning.

Oh, how I could fall in love with this man.

His thumb traces small circles on my skin. "We have all the time in the world to prove that to each other. But after—"

CLANK!

The metallic clang echoes above us, breaking up our moment. Cal grabs my hand and steps closer to the doors, pressing his ear against the seam. "Hang on," he mutters. "We're getting out of here." The elevator jerks, and we are moving down. Cal steps back, shielding me with his arm across my body.

I watch the numbers descend above our heads.

We pass L for Lobby.

And stop at Level A.

Chapter Eighteen
11:55 p.m.

Cal

The elevator jolts, a sharp metallic lurch that rattles the walls. My hand clamps tighter around the rail—and Rose.

With a grinding groan, the doors stutter open. We don't wait. We bolt.

Rose bursts out first, breathless. "Oh, thank God we're out of that death box!" she laughs, the sound shaky but real.

Her smile barely has time to settle before it fades.

Lights flicker weakly, revealing a vast concrete space, as the faint hum of generators and the echo of dripping water only add to the creepiness.

The lobby and rooms of the Black Onyx are stunning and polished. Which is what you'd expect from a high-end luxury hotel like this. The rest of the place, though? No, thank you. It's all eerie and almost unsettling.

And this basement is no exception.

"The bottom floor parking garage," I mutter.

Rose steps closer beside me, brow furrowing. "We wanted the lobby. I definitely didn't park here." She peers around me, taking in the scene before us. "Why would the elevator dump us out"—her nose crinkles—"here?"

"Guess the storm's messing with the system. Or maybe it's resetting itself." She hums in response. Neither of us moves.

As a cop, you know when danger is out there. It's like a quiet pressure that crawls under my skin and simmers long before any noise is made. Hell, I can smell it sometimes.

And right now, something stinks.

Outside this massive structure, thunder cracks, rolling along as the natural fireworks follow. Lightning flashes through the narrow windows, slicing white across the gray walls. Weirdly enough, the echo of the rain sounds heavier down here. It's pounding against the vents with its rhythm.

Rose shivers beside me. "Cal ... this is where they took her. We are in the same part of the garage, aren't we?"

I look over at her, catching the flash of pain and fear tightening behind her eyes. It hits me hard, sharp enough to make my own chest constrict. I hate this. I hate what she's been dragged through.

But I can't fall apart with her. Not now. My focus has to stay on finding her mom and ending this nightmare so that she can smile again. And—if the world gives us a damn break—we can figure out what we could be after all of this.

"Yes," I say quietly. "This is it."

She nods as the weight settles over her. I know what's running through her mind. The grainy video and the terror etched into every frame. Those images aren't leaving her anytime soon. I'm sure they will always haunt her. And standing here, watching her relive it all, makes me want to tear this entire garage apart until I find the truth.

Seeing her upset is doing things to me, so I have to take her away from here.

I grab her hand. "Let's get out of here. You okay getting back in the death box?"

"Haha, but also, heck no."

I chuckle. "Come on. We'll take the stairs. I'm not staying here a second longer than I have to. Stay close," I tell her, my tone sharp. It's a habit, I guess.

She laughs softly. "So bossy."

I glance back at her, and there's no stopping the smirk tugging at my mouth. "You love it."

Her cheeks bloom with that familiar shade of pink. It's funny—with us in this horrible situation, she manages to make my pulse skip.

Refocusing, I instinctively reach back for her. As our fingers lace, her hand squeezes mine. Should I be holding her hand while on duty? Probably not. But I think a lot of lines have been crossed at this point.

My free hand hovers close to my weapon as I scan the shadows crawling along the concrete. That familiar dread scratches beneath my skin again. Row after row of empty parking spaces stretch out ahead, with one or two parked cars scattered, dim lights above us dying like stars.

The garage is thick with the smell of oil, damp concrete, and something else I can't name. I tip my assessment upward, imagining the layers of this garage pancaked above us like slabs of steel and stone. Each floor is another angle for danger to hide. Something in the atmosphere is wrong. Off.

Unease pulses through every nerve in my body. I gotta get Rose out of here. Now.

"Let's not linger," I murmur, already steering her toward where I'm hoping the stairwell is.

But she slips out of my grip. "I want to see it," she pleads, tears trembling in her words. "The spot where she was taken. Please."

Her desperation hits me hard. And despite all my instincts screaming at me to move, I stop—because how can I deny her this?

Yet, I don't want her reliving what she saw on the video earlier. But I also know that determined look on her face all too well. So she pulls out the big guns and jets out her lower lip, giving me the ultimate pouty face. Again.

Damnit. My kryptonite.

Unable to say no to this woman, I huff, defeated. "Alright," I agree quietly, squeezing her hand. "But stay behind me."

We move deeper into the garage as our footsteps echo against the wet floor. The storm outside rages as thunder shakes the ceiling and pelting rain seeps in through open parts of the garage.

When we reach the far corner, she stops. Her eyes give away everything before she says a word. The recognition on her features morphs into sorrow and pain.

My heart breaks for her.

"This is it," she says, taking in the open space. Without warning, she sinks to her knees, trembling.

I crouch beside her, my hand settling on her shoulder. "Hey. Don't do this to yourself."

Tears slip down her cheeks as new ones linger on her long lashes, glinting in the dim light. Then she breaks. A strangled sob breaks free as her shoulders shake and the weight of this entire experience crashes down on her. "She was here, Cal. Right here." She points to the spot her mom was hovering on the dirty floor. "She was frightened and alone, and I wasn't—"

"Stop," I cut in gently. "Don't finish that sentence. This isn't your fault. We're going to find her. You hear me? We're going to bring her home." She turns away and a newfound determination fills me. With my fingers, I tug at her chin so that she's forced to look at me. "Let me rephrase that. *I'm* going to find her. I will overturn heaven and earth to bring her home to you. Do you hear me?"

And I will. Rose's happiness means the world to me.

She nods and slumps into me. Her smell assaults my nose as I wrap an arm around her, holding her steady, the weight of her grief pressing into me.

"But first we have to get out of this freaking creepy place, okay?"

"Okay," she agrees, nodding.

When she finally pulls back, I rise and offer my hand. Her fingers slip into mine, warm and trembling, and I draw her gently to her feet. The moment she's standing, she collapses against me. Her cheek rests over my heart as I wrap my arms around her, and she settles into my embrace. I kiss the top of her head, and let my hand drift through her brown, silky curls. "Let's go," she murmurs into my shirt, soft but certain. I ease her face back, brushing my thumb along her jaw.

"Now who's being bossy?" I ask, playfully. She laughs, the sound small and beautiful as I press a lingering kiss to her nose. It's enough to make her smile against the ache. And is exactly what I crave in this moment.

Faint footsteps come from the area to our left. My head snaps in the direction. Rose stands grabbing onto my forearm. "Did you hear that?" she asks. I nod as I scan the area again. Nothing's out of the ordinary. There are the puddles, the empty spaces, a few parked cars scattered, but nothing else. "I did. But I think it's clear."

I could have sworn I heard footsteps though.

With one last glance back at the scene of her mom's disappearance, Rose clenches my hand, and we start toward wherever this stupid stairwell is. The sound of the storm is still pounding above us.

As we pass the non-working elevator, movement jumps in my periphery. Something shifts in the shadows near the far wall.

"Stay behind me," I demand quietly, stepping slightly around Rose.

A shape emerges, slow and deliberate.

This isn't a hotel patron making their way to their car. Or someone arriving to get a late-night drink at the hotel bar. No, this is different. I narrow my eyes immediately, assessing the figure. It's a man. Tall, with broad shoulders and dressed in dark colors.

With calculated movements, he walks toward us. Instinct takes over; my hand hovers near my weapon, every sense locked on high alert.

Lightning flashes, and he comes into full view.

"Niko," Rose breathes as she steps around me. Multiple questions fill my brain and her face.

Why is he lurking around here?

Was he watching us?

Or following us?

He steps fully into the light, with water dripping from his clothes and hair. His expression is like stone, completely unreadable. Dread fills my whole body.

"Didn't expect to see you two down here," he says evenly. "Quite the storm, huh?"

But something in his tone sets my instincts off. My hand hovers and stays steady over my weapon. Rose inches closer to me, her body coiled tight.

Because I don't think Niko *happened* to be here.

Chapter Nineteen

One year prior

Niko

S he doesn't see me.

She never does.

Trying my hardest to stay concealed, I stand across the street beneath the shuddering blink of a broken lamppost, next to a bus stop. Its light cutting in and out like a heartbeat. Rain dots the bus-shelter glass, blurring my reflection, bending her shape into something ghostly and untouchable. The bar behind her throws a soft gold glow onto the sidewalk. She's alone now. Just her, the light, and the empty street.

She wasn't alone, though. For the last three hours, Cal Masters had her undivided attention.

Not me.

Him.

During the evening and with my baseball cap pulled low, I sat at the bar, keeping a comfortable distance to stay unnoticed as I watched.

I watched her bat her eyelashes at him.

I watched him touch her leg.

I watched her laugh at literally everything that came out of his mouth.

I watched it all.

I was so disgusted with the whole thing. But I had to keep my anger at her in check.

And how did I know she would be here tonight? Well, in case you haven't figured it out … I've been watching her. Making sure she's safe while also waiting for the right time to make a move.

I'm patient. I can wait for her to come to me.

Unlike that idiot. Cal walked away a minute ago.

How could he let Rose slip through his fingers? I thought for sure I would have to stoop to some pretty drastic measures if this turned into something between them.

But instead, he bolted on that obnoxious bike of his.

Ba-bye.

I saw how he leaned in, close enough for her to hold her breath. The way she waited. Her eyes closed as her chin tilted—expecting a kiss that woudn't come. When he pulled back, hurt flashed across her face. It was small and quick, but it hit me like voltage.

He doesn't deserve her.

No one does.

They don't see what I see.

Because Rose is different. She always has been. I knew it the first night we met. The way she laughed a beat too early, and how she studied people like she was taking them apart to see how they worked. She pretends she's fragile, but I know better. There's strength in her. Wild, unguarded strength.

And we trust each other.

At least, I thought she did.

I mean, of course, I knew she was shadowing him. I watched her walk into the station that first day and every day they worked together. So, he was definitely on my radar. Anyone who comes into her circle who is that handsome and a single guy, well, I have to keep tabs on them.

But she didn't *tell* me about Cal.

And that's when I knew she liked him.

We still talk. Daily.

There's texting and sometimes calls when the nights of writing get long for her. She doesn't know that I'm often closer than she thinks. While she talks, I stand at my usual perch across the street, just enough for me to see her clearly. She talks about her mom, how much she misses her dad, her writing, her dreams. Maggie. She knows I listen because of my big heart.

But I know more than she imagines.

I know where she goes when she's restless, which coffee shop keeps her favorite blend after hours. I know her routines, her shortcuts, the way her living-room curtain leaves a two-inch gap where the city light spills through. And how that window doesn't quite lock.

I know how she arranges her makeup and where she keeps the remote. I know how her sheets smell. And I know the perfect amount of treats to give her dog, Juno, to keep him quiet.

We're buddies.

So of course, I had to be here tonight.

When she told me she had plans, I had to come. Funny how the little flirt left out who she was meeting.

I needed to see, although I knew.

And now I have.

Cal left her behind; his strides were clipped, one hand brushing his jaw like he's second-guessing himself. He didn't turn back. Just got on that bike and rode away.

From Rose!

God, what a loser.

She stands unmoving. Hurt etches across her face as her arms wrap tight around her body. Her breath fogs in the cool night air as she stares down the street. Like she can still will him to turn around.

She won't call out. Please, I know my girl too well. Did you have any doubts?

That's when it happens. A realization clicks.

This is the moment.

This is my chance.

She's open and vulnerable now. Like a wounded animal.

And I can save her.

Me.

I'm the one.

I'll show her that someone's been paying attention all along.

I step off the curb, the lamplight dying behind me. Tires hiss through puddles as cars pass, spraying water over my shoes. The night reeks of wet asphalt and spilled whiskey from the bar's trash can. My distorted reflection ripples in the street, but I recognize the smile spreading there. I'm in control and certain.

By the time I reach the other side, I already know what to say. I've practiced every word. How they'll sound, how they'll land.

I know the exact warmth she'll hear in my voice, the kind that makes people drop their guard.

This isn't chance.

It's rehearsal meeting reality.

I slow my steps before she turns, already picturing the surprise in her eyes. There will be confusion at first. But then recognition, followed by relief.

Because she'll see me now.

She'll have to.

The way I've been waiting for her to.

She's mine now.

And this time, she won't walk away.

Chapter Twenty

12:09 a.m.

Rose

Lightning flashes through the small openings, painting Niko in brief, jagged light.

He's soaked, his hair dripping, his eyes—God, his ocean eyes—focus on me like he's seeing something he doesn't recognize. When we dated, I used to love to peer into those baby blues. His stare would always stir something inside me. I could get lost in them. But now, they are devoid of anything.

And scaring me.

"What are you doing down here?" I ask tightly. "I thought you were at the ball." *What time is it anyway?*

He shrugs far too casually. The movement is lazy and deliberate, and his eyes give him away. Cold and so calculating.

Unease creeps up my neck.

"It's over," he says, low as he inches closer, concrete crunching beneath his shoes.

Cal's hand tightens around mine, steady but tense. His other hand twitches over his gun. "I could ask you the same thing," Niko clips back. "Strange place for a date."

A date? What is he talking about? I told him why we were here. Didn't I? I blink, confusion flashing through me. "A what?"

His head cocks slightly, and his gaze drops to where Cal's hand wraps around mine. Niko stands, not answering me. Only staring. Which, somehow, is worse. The way his eyes linger and narrow unfurls something cold inside of me.

Cal doesn't speak, doesn't shift. But the slight change as his fingers tighten around mine lets me know he's here with me. The pressure is steady and deliberate. He's next to me, but dread surrounds us.

I scan the area, my heart pounding, hoping someone appears to chase Niko off.

But no one else is here.

The atmosphere is thick and tense; my nerves are frayed because something isn't right, and Cal is my only anchor.

"So," Niko says slowly, his face twitching, waving his finger between us. "You two a couple now?"

I yank my hand back, guilt slamming through me so fast it steals my breath. My pulse roars in my ears, drowning out everything else. It's like getting caught sneaking out with the boy down the street all over again.

Cal's eyes snap toward me, and I see the hurt before he masks it. We're not a couple—not officially—but we both know where this is headed. And the way I pulled away just now … it put a crack in something fragile, something we hadn't said out loud yet.

But I did it because Niko looked absolutely gutted when he saw us standing together. Instincts kicked in, and if I hadn't stepped back, I'm not sure what he would've done.

But I don't have time to fix it, or explain any of that to Cal. Not now.

Hostility rolls off him in waves. His gaze is like a weapon. "No," I start, the words shaky but firm. "It's not like that—"

He laughs, and the sharp, humorless sound reverberates against all my nerves. "You really expect me to believe that? I've seen you two."

Wait ... he's seen us. What does that mean?

Lightning flares again, and for a moment, his face is different. Harder, meaner. And a hell of a lot more scarier.

The tenderness I used to see there is gone.

The man who would hold me on the couch while we watched movies is gone.

The man who would stroke my arm while we drove in his truck.

Gone.

The man who promised me so much ... all of those versions of him.

Gone.

Who is the person before me?

But as fearful as I am right now, I have to keep my cool and hopefully bring back the Niko I knew.

Anxiety propels me forward as I move closer to him. Cal reaches for me. "Niko, what's going on with you?" I ask softly and carefully. "You're scaring me. You're not acting like yourself."

He advances, his voice rising and changing. "I'm scaring you?" In a split second, Cal is once again at my side, gripping my hand. Niko notices. "I've been trying to make you see me, Rose. You disappear with *him*, and now he's touching you like he owns you."

What is going on? Where is this coming from?

"Niko, I don't understand what you're—"

He cuts me off, eyes blazing. "I love you!"

The words crash over me louder than the thunder as they echo off the walls. I freeze. "You ... you what?"

"You heard me," he snaps. "I've always loved you, Rose. When we were together, I was waiting for you to say it first. And I tried so *damn* hard with you." He balls his hands into fists. "You didn't see it. Or maybe you didn't want to. At every turn, I showed you. But you were too busy writing your book, or spending time with your mom. Or perhaps still pining for him!" He jabs his finger toward Cal. "Then running off with people who don't give a damn about you. Like Maggie."

I recoil in shock at hearing her name. "Maggie? What does Maggie have to do with our relationship?"

My question hangs unanswered. I glance at Cal. He hasn't moved. He's right there, strong and steady. It's the only thing making me brave enough to stand here. Because this encounter with the person I thought I knew is forcing me to face a hard truth.

I wasted a year of my life.

Did I love Niko? Yes, but not enough to say it. And was that because of Cal? Maybe a little.

Okay, a lot.

But, any love I may have had for Niko, it wasn't with this version of him.

Because I remember.

My chest tightens as I throw it back at him. "You cheated on me, Niko! I know you did. I had my suspicions and no proof, but deep down, I knew. So you don't get to stand here and pretend like you loved me."

Something shifts on his face. The anger sharpens, twisting into something darker. "That wasn't cheating," he spits. "That was a mistake."

And there's the proof. But he's not done. "You—"

Cal steps around us, shielding me from Niko. "That's enough," he snarls out.

Niko's eyes snap to him. His hand twitches toward his jacket, reaching inside. "Stay out of this!"

Cal stiffens. "Don't do something you'll regret."

A boom of thunder rips through the garage as panic builds because this went from zero to a thousand in a split second. *What is Niko doing?*

Niko's hand flashes out, and I see the glint of metal before my brain catches up.

A gun.

"Cal!" I scream.

The next few seconds collapse in a blur. Cal jerks me back. The fluorescent lights flutter as the world seems to narrow to the three of us. He moves with impossible speed, and his gun is out, gripped in his hands as the barrel levels at Niko before I've fully registered the motion.

"Drop your weapon!" Cal's command reverberates off the pillars. Time speeds up and slows down simultaneously. How? No clue. Sounds all around us morph into one. The click of a safety, a distant car horn, the rain, the thunder. All of it surrounds us.

"Rose, get back!" Cal hollers, the command like a blade. Niko doesn't flinch right away. He stands his ground as his jaw works. Sinister attention cuts from Cal to me and back again. You can see it. Something dangerous brewing beneath the surface.

Cal's hand remains steady as he white-knuckles his weapon. He doesn't waver; every muscle screams control. "Don't come any closer," he commands.

Blood rushes fast and heavy, drumming through me. I want to say something—anything—but the words are stuck.

I am completely helpless. The seconds stretch into a drawn-out silence.

Niko doesn't listen to Cal's demands.

He pulls the trigger.

I scream.

Time stops.

The shot echoes, deafening in the enclosed space as concrete dust rains from the ceiling.

When you're in these types of situations, your mind thinks strange things. My first split-second thought before all hell breaks loose: *Is Niko a stormtrooper? Because his aim is terrible!*

Knocking me back to reality is Cal tackling Niko into the shadows. A gun clatters across the slick floor. I'm not sure if it's Niko's or Cal's.

"Run, Rose!" Cal yells, struggling to pin him.

I'm motionless. My body won't listen, but my instincts are screaming at me to flee. Heartbeats slam against my ribs as thunder muffles the clash of fists and rage coming from them both. I am gripped by fear, in shock and unsure of who will walk away.

Chapter Twenty-One

12:27 a.m.

Cal

The gunshot still echoes in my ears when I slam into Niko, the sound ricocheting through the parking garage like thunder trapped in concrete.

Whoever this weirdo was aiming for, it sure as hell wasn't me or Rose. He's a trigger-happy psycho who is obviously obsessed with my girl and whom I suspect has been stalking her. Not a good combo. And something else to add to my growing list of concerns today.

Our bodies collide, and we crash to the ground.

Hard.

We land on our sides as his skull bounces off the pavement and his gun skitters across the wet cement, spinning out of reach.

Thank God!

Niko's stronger than I expected. He's lean, wired, fast, and coiled up tight. Before I can register anything, he clocks me in the jaw with a wild punch that sends pain bursting behind my eyes. A searing jolt shoots through my neck as my head whips back from the impact.

This whole thing is frustrating the hell out of me because I am unable to get a hold of this guy. In a flash, I realize I don't know where Rose is. Panic rises, but I have to refocus. I manage to land a punch in his kidney. He grunts, which gives me the leverage I use to flip us both, landing him on his back. Providing me with the tiny window to find her.

Her frame comes into focus, standing near the elevator, hand clasped over her mouth, fear stretching across the features of her face.

"Rose, go! Get out of here!" I bark, but I don't know if she listens. My ears are ringing too loudly from the punch and the storm outside to hear anything.

Being distracted is all the opening Niko needs. He drives his shoulder into me, throwing me off balance once again. Okay, it's obvious this dude has had some sort of fight training because my back hits the floor hard, knocking the wind out of my lungs. On all fours, he scrambles for the weapon, his boots sliding in a puddle. We both stumble to stand at the same exact time.

Him racing for his weapon.

Me, determined to stop him.

Because I can't let him get that gun. His shot might be really bad, but all it takes is one good one to maim. Or kill.

And who would wind up dead? Rose? Not happening.

That thought alone lurches me forward. We are both standing now, making a beeline for his gun. I propel myself straight for him and manage to grab his arm and twist as he shouts. This time it's my boot that kicks the gun away as it clatters into the dark. With his foot, he lands a blow to my knee, and I cry out, releasing him from my grasp.

He twists around and for a minute, we're both still.

Breathing hard.

Circling each other.

Waiting.

Then he bolts.

"Damn it!"

Within seconds, I'm in pursuit, chasing after him. He sprints up the incline to the next level of the garage. From behind me, feet pound the pavement, and I'm almost certain it's Rose.

Of course, she didn't listen!

The storm outside flashes through the narrow openings—lightning tearing through the dark, thunder chasing right after it. My boots slap the wet floor, echoing off the concrete pillars as I pursue him. Empty spaces and parked cars whiz past me as I run after this guy. Who, apparently, is an Olympic sprinter with his speed.

"Niko!" I shout, but he doesn't slow as he veers to the left, disappearing around a corner.

"Cal!" Rose's wail—distant, frightened—cuts through the chaos. I spin around, heart pounding.

She's gone.

"Rose!" I'm sweating and disoriented. *Where did she go?*

The garage splits into two. One ramp to go up and one leading to the entrance of the garage from the street behind the hotel. I curse under my labored breath, frantically searching left and then right. Wondering where Niko went. And Rose. I've lost track of them both.

Through the exit door, next to the entrance, I glimpse a sudden movement. It's only a shape, half-swallowed by dark and a curtain of rain.

It's her. *Why is she going outside? What is she doing?*

Another, more desperate thought consumes me. *Is he following her now?*

My experience tells me I have to stay in pursuit of the lunatic who just shot at and assaulted a cop. But my heart is telling me to chase after the one woman who has affected me the way Rose has.

Hell, I might lose my job for this. Because it will be on camera. There's no hiding my feelings now.

Rain slams down in sheets the second I exit the garage. The wind howls, cold and relentless, slicing through my shirt. Lightning turns the sky white for a second at a time, before going black again.

"Rose!" I yell, fighting the noise.

Within seconds, I'm soaked to the bone. Water pours off my face, obstructing my view of the sidewalk. Swiping my hand down my features, I scan the area, and a figure comes into view a few yards away.

She's on the ground trying to get up and failing. As she clutches her ankle, her hair, heavy and wet, sticks to her face. Her clothes ... drenched through.

Something primal erupts in me. She's stranded, hurt, and wet.

And she needs me.

Adrenaline bursts out of me as I rush towards her. Every fiber of my being is propelling me forward.

To protect her.

Help her.

Save her.

I've never reached a victim so fast before. I grab her by the shoulders, hauling her up to a seated position.

"You okay?" I yell through the storm.

She nods weakly as her eyes flutter. She tries to blink away the rain pelting her eyes. Her whole body trembles. "I ... I fell." She grasps her foot. "I twisted my ankle."

"I got you." Sliding an arm under her knees, I lift her, cradling her against my chest. Her arms clasp around my neck as she clings to me, shivering while the rain pounds from above.

Her eyes snap to mine, huge and unsteady. "What about Niko?"

My lips move on their own and press a soft kiss to her temple. Despite the coldness of the rain, her skin radiates warmth. "You're the only thing that matters right now. I'm getting you out of here."

We move toward the back hotel entrance, away from the garage as the storm and rain howl, blurring everything. Rose grips my neck tightly, anchoring herself to me. As I walk, I squeeze her waist and pull her tighter against me. The lights of the hotel flash again, and for one fleeting second, I think we've made it.

The world explodes.

A gunshot.

The impact hits me before the sound registers. Then the pain. A burning punch to my shoulder, sharp and deep. My knees buckle, and I drop to the ground.

I've been shot, and the only thing going through my mind is: *Don't drop Rose.* Warm blood mixes with the icy rain streaming down my back.

"Cal!" Rose's scream cuts through the storm.

My knees smack the pavement hard, the shock of it ripping up my spine. The world tilts, blurring at the edges, and pain detonates through my shoulder and my side. I fight the darkness pressing in, threatening to pull me under as I clamp my teeth together from the pain.

Rose slips out of my arms, but before I can steady myself, the world tilts. *I'm going down.* But she's already there, catching me, pulling me into her lap before I hit the ground.

"Cal! No—Cal!" Her sharp scream slices through the fog. "Oh, my God!"

Her presence drags me back, but only halfway. My vision wavers, images swimming in and out of focus. I blink hard, trying to anchor myself to her, her hands, the emotion of her holding me together when my body can't.

A thought surfaces. *Is this the last time I will see her?* Because I have no clue how badly I'm injured.

So, before the world fades to black, I reach for her face and cup her cheek. Desperate to memorize every piece of her. My thumb grazes the arch of her brow, then trails lower, catching the rain gathered on her lashes. Her wide and brown eyes, locked on mine, are the last thing holding me here. I trace the bridge of her nose, committing the familiar shape to memory, then let my fingers drift down to her soft and warm lips. The same lips I finally got to taste. The memory of that elevator kiss flashes through my mind, bright against the darkness surrounding us.

I smile.

I absorb the details of her, storing them in my memory.

"Cal, please, don't leave me," she pleads as she leans down and presses the softest kiss on my lips.

I wince as I swing my arm around and grasp the nape of her neck, pulling her mouth to me.

She must sense my resolve, because she breaks free of the kiss and screams into the void. "HELP! Someone help!"

But, it all comes apart.

I see him.

Niko.

Emerging from the shadows. Rain streaming down his face. Focused and furious.

Niko shot me. *Boy, his aim improved at the perfect time, didn't it?*

Rose doesn't notice him at first, lost in her own world of panic.

"No one can hear you!" Niko grabs Rose by the arm, the shock of his arrival coursing through her as he drags her backward.

"NO!" she screams, kicking and fighting. But he's stronger. She reaches for me, clawing at the air, as she gets pulled further and further away.

I'm able to grab her ankle, but I lose my grip from the rain and loss of strength.

"Let her go!" I cry out, trying to push myself up, but pain rips through me like fire.

Niko glances back once; his face twists with something that doesn't register. A mix of jealousy, hate, and victory.

Probably all three. He smirks.

"CAL!" Her screams are like an arrow straight through my heart. "LET ME GO!" She's fighting, gripping the side door entrance to the hotel. Then, he shoves her through and disappears into the dark, pulling her with him.

The storm swallows her scream.

I crawl forward, hand pressed to my shoulder, blood slick against my fingers. "Rose!"

Only thunder answers.

Real genuine fear engulfs me. Because I've lost her.

I make a feeble attempt to stand as the pain in my shoulder radiates to my brain. Once I'm on my feet, I stagger once … twice …

… a few more times.

My vision blurs.

Then darkness.

Chapter Twenty-Two

2:17 a.m.

Cal

The world is black. Soundless, weightless. Then the pain drags me back.

Rain as cold as ice pelts my face, sharp as needles. My head throbs, and fire courses through my shoulder and arm. As if branded with a white-hot iron. When I lift my gaze, the fractured flashing caution light from the nearby intersection and the pulse from the storm are all I see.

I'm still on the sidewalk.

How did I get here?

My thoughts come in fragments.

Niko's gun.

Rose's scream as he took her.

The pain.

The sound of thunder swallowing her whole.

A low groan tears out of me as I try to move, and pain explodes through my shoulder. My opposite hand shoots up to clamp it, but the effort only makes it worse. Gritting my teeth, I push myself upright, my palm coming away from my shirt slick and warm with my blood.

Everything spins, edges blurring, before it finally steadies. Then another wave hits. This one's sharp as splitting pain radiates from the back of my skull. I reach up, fingers brushing over my hair until they find the same familiar sticky goo. More blood.

I must have blacked out, fallen, and smacked my skull on the ground. There's nothing but the cold and wet pavement where my head was resting, with no sign of blood.

The rain has already washed most of it away.

"Rose…" Her name leaves my lips in a broken rasp. I survey the scene: an empty street, that same annoying flashing light buzzing overhead, and puddles reflecting the somber, gray sky.

No sign of her.

No sign of him.

I drag myself to my feet, bracing against the side of the building. Is this the parking garage? I'm not sure. My bearings are off. With shaking hands, I pull out my phone from my back pocket and, miraculously, it's still intact.

The screen glows. **2:17 a.m.**

Two hours.

Two damn hours since I was shot.

Two hours since she was taken.

So much can happen in two hours.

I scroll through my contacts, press the phone to my ear, and call the one person I can trust.

"Cal," Denny answers before the first ring finishes

"It's me," I manage, roughly and wet with rain.

"Jesus, where are you? I've been calling you for the last hour. I assumed you were still stuck in the elevator. You sound like hell."

"She's gone," I choke out. "Niko … he took Rose. He shot me. I'm outside the garage near the back of the hotel."

Silence hangs as Denny processes. "Who in the hell is Niko? Never mind." I can hear the unspoken compassion in his voice on the other end. "You're hit? Where? How bad?"

I glance over at my wound and the hole in my shirt. "My shoulder. It went clean through. I'll live, but I think I've lost a lot of blood," I mutter, pressing harder against the wound. "Plus, I hit my head. I probably have a concussion." I squeeze my eyes, testing out my self-diagnosis. Everything blurs and then focuses slowly. I was right. "But we can't waste any time. He's got her, and we're already behind."

"Alright," Denny says, switching into command mode. "You're hurt, so stay where you are. I'm sending units and an ambulance. We'll get you patched up, then we'll start the search. You hear me? Don't move!"

"I'm not waiting," I snap, forcing myself upright. The world spins, but I hold steady. "He's got a two-hour head start, and if he's working with someone—"

"Cal." Denny's control cuts through hard. "If you go down again, you're no good to her. Stay put."

I close my eyes, fighting the urge to throw the phone. The rain pounds harder, washing the blood from my hands.

For once, I do as I'm told.

I sink back against the wall, clutching my shoulder, listening to the thunder fade into the distance.

But in my memory, all I can hear is her calling my name as she was dragged away.

And I swear to God, I won't stop until I get her back.

With all the strength I have left in me, I push off the brick.

And race straight for the door he took her through.

Chapter Twenty-Three

1:32 a.m.

Rose

A voice.

"Rose. Sweetheart, wake up."

It's soft. Familiar.

I blink through the haze. There's an ache behind my eyes, and my wrists burn. After a second, it clicks. Zip ties bite into my skin, anchoring me to a chair. The room is dim and smells faintly of disinfectant and burning plastic. Which is odd.

Then I see her.

"Mom?" My question cracks, disbelieving.

Is this a dream? Am I dreaming?

A fuzzy vision of her morphs and takes shape. It's white and blurry, but it's her. I blink tightly once and then twice, trying to clear what's clogging my vision.

Slowly, things are starting to make sense.

Mom sits across the room, her face ghost-pale, wrists bound tightly behind her. For a moment, I forget how to breathe. But then her eyes meet mine, and relief floods her face.

She's still in her ballgown. The fabric's torn and frayed at the hem. Her once-elegant hair hangs in tangled, greasy strands around her face, matted against her cheeks. The dark circles reveal her exhaustion, but she's here—*she's alive.* Tears cloud my vision as her lips tremble into a smile. "Oh, thank God," she breathes out.

"M... Mom." The word scrapes out of me as the sight of her hits me so hard my whole body goes numb. Tears burn up instantly, blurring my reality. "I ... I thought you were—"

The rest dies in my throat. I can't say the word *dead.* I won't. Not when she's right here. Alive! And looking at me with the same disbelief and aching relief tearing through my body.

"I know," she whispers. "I know, sweetheart. I'm here. I'm alive."

Hearing her say it causes all the unease I've been holding in to leave my body. I smile, and a relieved laugh slips out. I want to prove to myself that she's real and throw my arms around her, run to her, surround myself with her motherly affection. And I know she wants to do the same.

But we can't. Both of us unable to move, tied to our chairs. The distance feels like miles and not feet. It's unbearable.

My hands twitch uselessly behind my back, aching to hold her. Instead, all I can do is sit here and let the relief crash through me in one overwhelming wave.

But then the fear returns as my body tenses, remembering why I'm here in the first place. Cal holding me, the gunshot, Cal falling, the rain. So much rain. The images race back, and my body chills. "Cal," I squeak out with a shiver. "He was shot. He ... he tried to protect me."

Mom's tired face fills with nothing but sympathy and the motherly affection I missed so much these last few days. "Cal?" she asks softly. "Is he the one you worked with last year? The guy you really liked?" She trembles at the memory. There's a faint, knowing smile on her lips. As only a mother can have.

She remembers. Of course she does.

I told her everything.

How Cal made me feel seen for the first time.

How I was falling for him. Hard.

How it broke me when he walked away that night.

She knows it all. I nod, a tear slipping down my cheek. "I've been with him all night, Mom. Trying to find you. He's been working on your case." I pause. "Those feelings didn't go away. Cal is … well, he's amazing. He…" Choking, I'm unable to get the rest out as the sobs overwhelm me. The thought of never seeing him again coupled with not knowing if we could make it work, rips through me.

"They'll find him. If he's as strong as you described to me last year, he will be okay. But right now, you need to stay calm. Do you hear me? *Trust* me when I say that you *have* to stay calm."

She says this as if she knows something I don't.

Tears track my cheeks as I nod while forcing a breath, glancing around. *Where are we?* Wires run across the floor, snaking into black boxes stacked against the walls. Monitors skip and flash with half-dead screens. Security feeds, maybe. I'm not sure.

For a second, the image of the lobby flashes, distorted by static.

Then it hits me. "Oh, my God." I blink at the screens again, the tangled setup of routers and laptops. "This is surveillance equipment. These are images of the hotel."

Mom nods faintly. "They moved me here after you arrived. This room is bigger. I was in the one next door."

"Niko took me. He drugged me with something. He's the one who shot Cal. Why would he bring me—" Then my mom's words register. "Wait. *They?*" I echo.

Her brows knit together as her expression softens. "Rose, honey—" But before she can say anything, the door swings open.

Niko steps in first. His clothes and hair are still damp from the rain.
Anguish carves deep into his features. My stomach lurches as soon as I
see him.

And then she walks in.

Maggie?

For a heartbeat, I don't breathe. Her face is assured, but her eyes give
her away. They're sharp, irritated, almost … annoyed.

My jaw drops.

No. No, no, no—this can't be right. Maggie's in Italy right now.

Flashes of the last few hours play on a loop like a movie. I think back
to our FaceTime earlier today and immediately recognize the window
across the room. The soft white curtain. The brick wall outside. How
she held the phone, blocking my view of her room. My mind works
backwards as I remember hearing rain when we talked. I glance into
the bathroom. The same one she was in during our call.

She was at the hotel the whole time. In this very room.

Then the commotion, and she told me she was at a club. The Mask.
She was at the ball.

Mom's note.

It all makes sense. Mom didn't know who was chasing her. She
thought she was going to die and wanted Maggie to know she was sorry
about the night of the fire.

But now?

My mind trips over itself. Is she part of this? Is she involved? Or—is
Niko forcing her? Is she trapped too?

None of it fits or makes sense. My thoughts spin, smashing into each
other, desperate for a version of this moment that isn't true. But the
longer I look at her, the more the truth becomes my reality.

The room tilts, sounds fading in and out as the pieces come together
in ways I don't want to see. Questions claw their way through my mind.

How long?

Why?

What did I miss?

And why is she with Niko?

Every memory, every conversation with her, suddenly feels tainted. I can't tell what's real anymore. Only that nothing is steady. The room blurs slightly then focuses. Whatever was on the cloth Niko put over my mouth is still lodged in my head.

Niko locks onto me instantly. "Rose." He crosses the room in three long strides and kneels beside me, glancing around, assessing the zip ties, upset and concerned that I'm strapped to this chair. Which is ... confusing. He reaches for me, but I reel back as far as I can. "Are you okay? I know you must me so mad, but I had to—"

I jerk to the left. "Don't touch me."

He blinks, startled.

Behind him, Maggie's jaw clenches. "Unbelievable," she mutters. "Even now."

The bite in her tone borders on hatred. My brain stalls, refusing to make sense of it all.

"Maggie," the name tastes like ash as everything finally clicks. "You... you're behind this?"

She smirks, stepping into the light, and bows. She freaking bows. "Took you long enough."

"Why?" The question trembles with disbelief. "Why would you do this?"

Maggie catches the way my expression crumples, the way realization hits me like a blow. She sees it.

And she's enjoying it.

A cruel little smile twitches at the corner of her mouth as she takes pleasure in the damage she's caused. "Because I hate you," she spits, the words cutting like glass. More shock. More confusion. "I always have. You had it all. The attention, sympathy, love. Even my parents liked you better."

I watch her, stunned. "Your parents? What are you talking about? Are you high? On drugs? Maggie ... it's me and Mom," I plead, hoping to snap her out of this and bring back *my* Maggie.

But the words don't register. "Don't act shocked," she sneers. "You know what they did. You just don't know *why*. They were taking what they deserved. Your mom ruined them."

Denny was right. Maggie's parents were thieves, stealing people's identities. And my mom figured it out and confronted them that tragic night.

I glance at mom, ready to ask what happened, but she's zeroed in on Maggie. Her voice quivers from across the room. "They ruined themselves, Maggie. How many more times do I have to say it?"

Maggie whirls on her. "You took everything from me!"

"They did that to themselves! I tried to save them. They wouldn't listen."

"It doesn't matter how many times you say it, Diane. It won't be enough or bring them back!"

My attention pings between them, trying to keep up. The animosity is thick, heavy with something that feels old. It's clear this isn't their first fight.

What *happened* in this room? It's obvious something awful has already taken place, and I've been dragged into the aftermath. The weirder this gets, the harder it is to piece it together and the more everything slips through my grasp.

Niko stands abruptly, facing Maggie. "This isn't helping." He rests his hand on her shoulder, then his thumb rubs against her shirt. The gesture is almost sweet.

Caring.

My glance darts from him to her, the realization cutting through me like a knife. "You're working together."

Maggie's lips curl into a cold smile. "Oh, we're *more* than that."

Bitterness reaches my tongue. "What?"

Niko's guilt-ridden eyes say it all.

"You," I snarl to Maggie. "You're the one he cheated with."

This cannot be happening. Maggie. My cousin. My best friend. The one person I trust more than anyone … slept with Niko. Why? *Why would she do that to me?*

I dig my heels into the hard floor. God, I need Cal right now. *Where is he? Is he okay?*

Maggie doesn't deny it. Only smiles. "Of course you didn't notice. How he looked at me. How bored he was with you."

"Maggie," Niko warns through clenched teeth, but she doesn't flinch. Her eyes spark with something dangerous—something that almost borders on delight. Then he turns to me, and his expression softens. "I wasn't bored with you, Rose," he says sweetly, the words sliding out like poison dressed as a half apology.

My mom scoffs from her chair, but the sound barely registers.

Maggie laughs mockingly. "Seriously, Niko? You're still obsessed? How pathetic." Her smirk deepens. "I'd say, after everything, that ship didn't just sail—it sank."

Niko shoots her a piercing glare.

But me? I'm searching for the friend I used to know, instead all I find is hatred. It burns as if she's been waiting years for this moment. Every word, every glance is like a deep cut that won't heal. This isn't my Maggie. That girl is gone. This is someone darker and colder. Someone who's enjoying watching me suffer and hurt. And yes, I want to understand where this is coming from. But also, a part of me doesn't.

Not anymore.

She continues to spew her venom. "All your perfect little smiles, your good-girl act. God, it made me sick." She points to herself. "It was time to take some things for myself. So I thought, why not start with him? But of course, he felt all bad and didn't want to keep it going. And once again, I lost. To you." She breaks into an evil smile. "But then he broke it off with you anyway, out of guilt, so I was happy."

Niko's still trained on me, waiting for me to respond.

I hear my mom's words from earlier. *You need to stay calm. Trust me when I say that you have to stay calm.*

So I do. I keep my face impassable, refusing to act hurt or dejected from all this betrayal.

He drops to his knees as if he's about to beg. Probably for understanding or, worse yet, forgiveness.

He won't find either.

His shoulders sag as if the words themselves are too heavy. "It meant nothing, Rose. Nothing. It was harmless fun. She was throwing herself at me, and I'm a man! You understand, right? You're my world, Rose. I love you."

I'm stunned into silence as I stare, struggling to process what he just said. Those last three words come out as more of a plea than a declaration, as if saying them will change my mind.

They won't.

"When did it start?" And why do I care? Niko and I aren't a couple. At this point, I have no idea what I saw in him. I never thought he was capable of this.

He stands as Maggie encircles him with her arms, snuggling into his side, but he doesn't return the affection. His arms hang limp. "Go ahead. Tell her." She kisses his cheek.

He flinches away from her touch, eyes dropping to the floor. The movement is small, but it's enough. The sting hits Maggie's face before she has a chance to hide it. He won't look at me, his muscles shifting as if he's holding something back. Something he doesn't want to admit.

"Yeah, Niko. Tell me. *Please*," I mock. "I'm *dying* to know."

Do I want to find out how both my ex-boyfriend and best friend betrayed me while held against my will by those same two people?

Of course not. However, he's really uncomfortable right now. And I want him to feel every ounce of that unease.

But he doesn't answer. His mouth opens, then shuts again. Before he can find the words, Maggie cuts in. A slow, knowing smile curves on her lips. She's savoring this. "I knew he wouldn't be able to resist. No man could. You wouldn't understand," she purrs, her tone silky and deliberate. "You didn't see how he wanted me when you weren't around."

Her gaze sharpens, that smug smile hardening at the edges. I look to him, desperate for denial, but he turns away—guilt written on every line of his face.

"It started small and friendly," she continues, "a few texts, a drink here and there. You were too busy chasing your perfect life to notice. And by the time you did, it was already too late."

I want to vomit. "You're right, Maggie. I don't understand how you could betray me like that."

"And I would do it all over again to see you looking the way you do right now." Her smile borders on sinister. She shrugs while casually examining her nails. "Who knows? Maybe Cal will like what he sees once he meets me."

His name on her tongue sends rage through every nerve in my body. "Do not even *think* about him. Don't say his name!"

She tilts her head to the ceiling. "Oh, I'm thinking about him all right." She giggles.

Oh, my God. She has lost her mind.

"Enough," Niko snaps, running a hand through his wet hair. "Maggie, stop. Your vendetta and this act aren't helping right now, so would you just keep your head on straight. And Rose is right. Don't say *his* name. I can't have her thinking about him!" He says this like I'm not right here. *Because, Niko, sir, Cal is all I'm thinking about right now.*

As if he can read my thoughts, he shoots me a glare that screams annoyance. If looks could kill, I would be dead.

Maggie rolls her eyes, crosses her arms, and plops down on the bed like a child.

Niko continues. "Besides, the power outage ruined the feeds. They are unstable now, and the remote systems are down." He points to the hotel room door. "I have no clue what's going on out there. If we don't get access soon—" His words stop on his tongue as he sits in front of one of the monitors, typing on a keyboard.

Niko is a total computer geek.

The whole time we were together, I knew he worked in IT. He loved computers, anything tech-related really. All of it was way too big for my brain, but I loved the nerd it brought out in him. He would sit at his computer, working away, his glasses resting on the bridge of his nose, tongue jetting out in concentration.

He was impossibly cute and irresistible.

Now, the thought of being attracted to that is making me want to puke.

A few times, he would show me how he could breach certain companies' servers. It was wrong of course, but I think he liked knowing he could. Being the supportive girlfriend I was, I would ooh and ahh at his skills. He loved the validation. It made him feel in control and important.

"You mean you can't keep manipulating the hotel's security," I cut in, thinking back to when we watched the footage of him taking my mom. How images of an empty garage would cut in periodically. "You've been watching. Haven't you? That's why you showed up in the lobby. You saw me walk in." It all makes sense now. "It was all you. The mix-up with cleaning my mom's room. The feed cutting out when you chased her—"

"—the fake security footage so no one would see me taking her, forcing the elevator to stop at the basement so I could confront you," he continues. "I have control of the whole system from here. It took a ridiculous amount of planning. Pretty impressive, huh?" he asks, almost as if he craves my praise.

I think he seriously wants to impress me. *What a psycho.*

"You could see everything." I draw out the words because I'm far from impressed. I'm disgusted.

Niko's jaw tightens, a muscle twitching as he slowly turns toward me, shaking with fury. Gone is the man who was remorseful and saying he's in love with me. "Oh, I saw more than enough," he growls. "I saw him pin you up against that pillar in the garage. I saw every stare, every touch, every time he couldn't keep his eyes or hands off you. You think I didn't notice the way he watches you?" His words come faster, sharper. "But then the ball—seeing you with him in person—watching you *hold* him. You let him touch you!" He laughs, bitter and broken. "How could you hold another man like that?"

My blood spikes. "Me? Are you kidding? We aren't dating anymore, Niko," I snap. "You slept with someone else! Maggie!"

His eyes flash. "I told you that was a mistake!"

Pure disgust twists tighter the more he talks. The thought of him watching me.

Watching *us.*

It makes my skin crawl. He's been behind those cameras, taking in every stolen glance, every near touch between Cal and me.

Without warning, a thought sparks, and I grin. If the feeds went down, he didn't see what happened in the elevator.

I lift my chin, meeting his glare head-on. "So you didn't see us in the elevator?

He stiffens. "W ... what do you mean?"

I smirk. "Hmm ... that must have been when the feeds cut out. It's too bad, really," I say, steady, defiant. "You would've gotten a real show."

He lunges toward me, fury radiating off him. His face twists as every ounce of restraint disappears. My words hit the mark, and now the possibilities spinning in his imagination are eating him alive. "You slut!" he shouts, trembling with rage. "You think this is funny?!"

He's towering over me, breathing hard.

I force myself still. "If the truth hurts that much," I say quietly, "maybe you should've thought about that before sleeping with my cousin."

His jaw locks as his hands curl into fists. There's a war raging deep inside him. Supposed hurt because of his love for me versus the horror of what he's become.

He spits out his next words, low and venomous, meant to cut me. "I should have killed your mother in that garage when I had the chance."

"Then do it," Mom commands, trembling through the chaos. Fragile and fierce. She hasn't uttered a word until now. "Kill me and let Rose go. Please."

"Mom, no!" I plead, sharp and desperate. Pain sears through me, but I don't have time to breathe before everything shifts.

Maggie turns, her face hardening like stone. "Rose isn't going anywhere."

Chapter Twenty-Four

2:38 a.m.

Rose

The storm outside is fading into the distance, but it's still a constant roar. Remnants of any lingering rain tap the window. Minutes have passed without anyone talking. Niko continues to hammer away at the computer.

I'm still wrapping my brain around the fact that he was the masked man in the video.

He's a monster.

Maggie is lying on the bed, staring at me. Everything about this whole situation appears warped and unreal.

Yet, the hate I see in Maggie is very real.

I lock eyes with her and shift in my seat attempting to get a little more comfortable. The ties dig further into my wrists. "What's your endgame here, Maggie?" The question comes out low, steady, despite the panic clawing at me. "You've had my mom all this time. If you're still angry about the fire, then why haven't you killed her yet?"

Maggie turns her head, and her mouth curves. "Because that would've been too easy," she says softly. She sits up, swinging her legs and sitting on the edge of the bed. "I wanted you to see it, Rose. To *feel* it. To understand what it's like to lose everything. The way I did."

My adrenaline spikes. *Did I hear that right?* She wants me to *watch* her take my mom's life. "You're insane," I accuse, breaking through the rising panic.

Her smile falters, and she pauses briefly. It's clear she's enjoying this, but deep inside her, something is hesitating.

And in that brief moment, I see it. The tiniest fracture beneath all the hate. Because as much as Maggie wants to hurt us, she's fighting herself. Every breath tells me she's torn in two.

Rage pulling one way.

Love pulling the other.

This isn't just vengeance. It's pain and grief that's twisted into something she can barely control. She wants to end it, to finish what she started ... but deep down, I think some part of her still remembers who we were. And that's the only thing keeping us alive.

I search the room, desperate. There's no weapon, no escape.

Nothing.

They've inflicted enough damage on my mom, and I have to keep them from hurting her anymore. But how? The only option I have left is to keep her talking. Keep *them* talking. To stall. And maybe if I push hard enough, I'll get the truth out of them before it's too late.

Starting with Niko. I glance in his direction. He's now abandoned his perch with the monitors and is against the wall near the window. His arms are crossed as he stares outside, his jaw tight. "And what about you?" I ask, trembling. "Why are you here, Niko, helping her? You two aren't in a relationship anymore. So what do you stand to gain with all of this? Because if you thought this would make me love you, you are just as delusional as she is."

He looks at me, truly looks, and something shifts across his face. "Because she promised me money," he says quietly. "A lot of it."

The words hit like a slap. "Money?"

Maggie laughs. "It's simple, really. My plan took shape when digging through your"—she directs this to my mom—"office one day. And I found your will. Of course, it said that if you croak, dear Rose here gets everything with a little left over for me. Well, I couldn't let that happen, now, could I?" She's pacing now as she speaks. "But if you both die, well, it all passes to moi." She points to herself, fluttering her eyelashes.

My insides twists. "You're going to kill us for *the inheritance?*"

She shrugs. "Call it poetic justice. Plus, you'll both be out of my life for good, so that's an added bonus."

Distant thunder rattles the windows again, a flash of lightning illuminating Niko's face. He's pale, eyes darting, jaw tight. He pushes himself off the wall. "Hold on. Getting rid of Rose wasn't part of the deal."

The conflict is there—the hesitation. He's not as far gone as she is.

Maggie lifts a shoulder in defiance. "Plans change."

In two long strides, he charges at her, standing inches from her face. "No! I agreed to help you get rid of Diane. You promised you would split your inheritance with me and then leave Rose and me alone. And it's not *a little bit* of money. You don't need it all. Why are you being so greedy?"

Pretty sure greed isn't the only problem right now, Niko.

Maggie flips her arms, slamming them on her thighs. "Well, that was before you decided to take Rose! Kinda put a wrench in our plans, don't you think. Because now, she will go to her new police boyfriend, you idiot. And all because you got jealous and possessive seeing her with Cal!"

"He's not her boyfriend!" Niko screams out.

As they argue, I lock eyes with my mom. Her lips part as if she wants to speak, but nothing comes out. Her pale jaw trembles with terror, and yet she manages a small, broken smile. An attempt to comfort me when she's the one who's terrified. She's trying so hard to hide it from me. But I see it.

Her face tells me what words can't. Fear, love, and the quiet acceptance of someone who knows time is running out. The dim light of the room catches her eye, and for a moment, I see my mom as she's always been. Brave, stubborn, and unbreakable.

A newfound resolve bubbles forth within me. *Our lives are not ending in this room.*

Niko straightens. "I love her. I won't lose her to him. You know this."

Maggie studies him for a long moment, shoves her palm in his face, then hisses. "I can't with you. I'm going out to get some air." She turns and strides to leave the room, muttering under her breath as she whips open the door and disappears.

The door clicks shut behind her.

Now there's only me, Niko, Mom, the hum of the computers, the faint rattle of rain. My pulse thunders in my ears.

This is it. I steal a look at my mom, and she nods. It's like she knows my intentions and what I'm about to do.

"Niko," I implore softly. "Look at me."

He does. And for a moment, I see the man I used to know—the one who made me laugh, the one who wooed me under the streetlights and made me so many promises.

"There has to be another way. Don't listen to her," I implore. "We can leave. You and me. I have plenty of money, so we'll disappear. We can still fix this. Without hurting my mom. She'll stay silent if you just let us go."

"It's true," Mom chimes in. "I won't say anything. I'll even help. Tell me how much you would need to start over. Money's no object."

"See!" I watch him closely as the weight of my words sinks in. His jaw tightens, his breath falters, and for a second, it looks like he might agree.

But then his shoulders sag, defeated. "You'll never forgive me," he murmurs, the words cracking under their own regret.

"I already have." I force out the lie, steady and calm. "You made a mistake. I get it. I was only pretending to be mad at you because of Maggie. She's crazy. I didn't want her to see the love that still exists between us. But if you let me go, we can start over."

He studies me. I continue. "I understand why you took me from him."

Suspicion and longing are warring in his eyes. "You mean that?"

"Yes," I nod while trying to ignore the bile rising. "Niko, I need you." I almost choke on the next lie. "I love you."

He closes his eyes and exhales as soon as I say those three little words. As if he's waited an eternity for me to declare them. He steps closer. "What about *Cal*?" he asks with bite.

I shake my head. "He means nothing to me, I swear. Getting your texts and then seeing you in the lobby stirred up so many emotions. It made me realize I missed you, and he was … there. Like Maggie was for you." I force a weak smile. "But you took care of him, right? He's not a problem anymore." The thought of Cal bleeding out on that sidewalk wounds me deeply, but I bite it back, holding tight to my mom's words.

Stay calm.

Another step closer. "Promise me."

I'm suffocating. "I promise. It's just us. You and me."

His hand lifts slowly, fingers tracing the side of my face. The touch is heartbreakingly gentle, like I remember. Yet, cruel in its tenderness.

He hinges forward and his lips meet mine.

The urge to recoil hits hard. My body is itching to shove him away, to scream, to run.

But I don't.

I can't.

If I want us to live, I have to let him.

The kiss starts soft and hesitant before turning desperate. He tastes like rain and regret ... and something darker that seeps under my skin.

He pulls back slowly, looking relieved. Happy. His breath trembles. "I still love you," he sighs out slowly.

With his words still hanging and unbalanced, the door flies open.

Damnit!

Maggie stands frozen and unmoving, framed by the hallway light.

She saw the kiss.

Nobody moves. Nobody breathes.

Then she lifts the gun.

"I was gone for what, three minutes, and the first thing you do is run to her," she snaps, with anger coiling around her. "God, you're pathetic."

She steps further into the room, gun still outstretched. "And now, because of the little kidnapping-shooting-an-officer stunt you pulled, the police are here." She unlocks the safety. "I'm putting an end to this. To all of you. Right now."

Chapter Twenty-Five

2:38 a.m.

Cal

I don't like the vibe in the lobby. Everything about this whole God-forsaken fancy pants hotel feels wrong now that Rose is gone.

Rain continues to pelt the windows as distant thunder from the fading storm shakes the glass. The entire lobby is now swarming with police. The EMT's insisted that I go to the hospital for my wounds, but I refused. I'm not leaving this hotel until I have answers about what Niko did with my Rose. On top of that, her mom is still missing. And I'm one hundred percent sure Maggie and now Niko are involved with both.

The betrayal Rose must be experiencing has to be unbearable. My aching heart throbs along with my bandaged shoulder, but sitting idle isn't an option. Every minute that passes is another she's gone. And in danger.

Today wasn't supposed to go this way. The circumstances were utter chaos. But for a few hours, she was back in my world. We'd made quiet promises to each other. To see what might happen once this was over.

And now, the thought of losing her again twists my gut, sharp and relentless.

But it also ignites something in me. Because if Rose is out there—hurt and terrorized—then I'll tear this city apart to bring her back.

My phone chimes from my back pocket. It's Denny. I answer. "I'm waiting for security," I bite into the phone. All niceties are gone.

"Good. My ETA is about ten minutes. Nothing yet?"

"No."

"We will find her ..." He trails off as the elevator dings, and Mr. Hawkins rushes across the lobby toward me, face pale.

"Denny, hang on. He's approaching now. Don't hang up. I'm putting you on speaker." I hit the button.

"Detective ... thank ... goodness ... you're still here," he says, breathless and relieved.

"Yeah." I stand, ignoring the pain. "I have my superior on the line as well. Tell me you've got something."

He nods, practically becoming an asthmatic right before my eyes from the sprint here. This urgency is a good thing, though. I like this guy and will settle for zero incompetence when it comes to finding Rose. "We've been reviewing the system logs. The entire hotel's network—security cameras, elevator controls, card readers—it's all been compromised."

My gut tightens. "You mean, like what? Hacked?"

"Yes, sir. Someone's been inside our system for weeks, rerouting feeds, locking cameras, falsifying timestamps. This was a pretty extensive and calculated attack that was hidden really well. We still would be in the dark if it weren't for this storm and the outage."

"You hearing this, Denny?" I ask into the phone.

"Loud and clear."

Mr. Hawkins gestures toward the computers behind the front desk. "We recovered one partial feed before the rest cut out again."

I follow him around the counter, my nerves on edge. The monitor comes to life, the image grainy but clear enough: Niko, half-dragging, half-guiding Rose down a narrow corridor. She's struggling, fighting. He yanks a rag from his back pocket and covers her mouth with it. Her fight slowly fades. Then she goes limp in his arms. He carries her out of view.

Something ugly detonates in my chest, hot and blinding. I lock my jaw, forcing myself to breathe. "Where is that?" I snap.

"Old maintenance wing," he explains. "Hardly anyone goes there. It's not on the public floors."

My pulse spikes. "Get me there. Now."

"Wait for me, Cal!" Denny warns through the phone. I ignore him.

"There's one more thing," Mr. Hawkins bites out as he types on the keyboard. The feed for the hallways of fifteen floors fills the screen, each with its own box. They cut out and then back in again due to the unstable connection. But one is blank.

"Why is floor fifteen blacked out?" I ask, pointing to the screen.

"We are trying to get the feeds back up and out of the hands of whoever is doing this. But this floor. We've been unable to connect to it. But we managed to find something."

My stomach bottoms out. "What?"

He swallows. Hard. "Our surveillance is still weak, but we regained access to our booking system. The person behind this made it appear as if every room on that floor was booked. So if someone online, including our front desk, attempted to reserve a room with us, the system would default to another floor. That floor has been unoccupied for three days. Except for two adjoining rooms."

"How do you know this?" Heat crawls up my neck as his words stoke the fire under my skin.

"Like I said, we regained access to a few things. Room access being one of them." He moves over one workstation to another computer and types. "Here's a log of the room entries on that floor for the past three days."

I scan the screen, and two-room numbers repeat over and over. Room 1518 and 1520.

Denny isn't here, but he knows me all too well. "Cal, stand down. That's an order."

I jam my finger onto the end button, hanging up on my boss.

"Give me a key," I bark out.

He whips his lanyard from his collar and hands it to me. "Here, this opens every door in this building."

I don't hesitate and sprint around the desk with only one goal in mind. Get to Rose.

"Do you need help?" Mr. Hawkins's words trail after me, but I ignore him as I sprint through the lobby, my feet moving faster than my brain.

It's unthinkable. Niko has Rose here. Right here in this hotel.

I'm not waiting around for help and backup to get organized. The storm outside echoes through the walls, pushing me faster and harder until I reach the main elevator. My finger repeatedly jams the up button as I look at the digital floor reader above my head. Both elevators are on the upper floors.

I slam my hand against the wall. "Damnit."

No time. I pivot and shove through the stairwell door, pounding up the steps two at a time, using the rail to hurl myself forward. Pain flares in my shoulder, sharp and relentless as I pass floor after floor. Fresh blood seeps through the bandage. I ignore it.

Every second counts.

When I finally reach the fifteenth floor, my head is ready to explode and the dizziness starts. But I push that aside as I shove the door open, and the sound echoes down the hallway. With quick movements, I attempt to get my bearings. The hallway stretches out before me, long and empty.

Completely silent.

I draw my gun, the familiar weight grounding me as my finger rests outside the trigger guard.

To my right—Room 1501. *Crap!* It's all the way at the far end. I control my steps, but move quickly. With all of my senses heightened, I angle my gun low, ready to fire. I'm tracking every shadow, every door as I tune into the smallest sound.

I reach Room 1518 first and press my ear to the door.

Nothing except for the low hum of the lights above me.

Two quick steps bring me to 1520.

That's when I hear it.

Voices.

Then one cuts through clear enough to stop my breath. Rose.

"Maggie, please, no! Don't do this!"

That's enough for me. Adrenaline hits hard and quick. I draw in one steady breath, brace myself, tap the badge, and kick the door open.

My eyes sweep the room, fast and frantic. It's dimly lit and heavy with heat and panic. Wires snake across the floor, monitors flittering with static and grainy feeds of the hotel. Diane's bound to a chair, pale and trembling. Rose is too. With Niko standing beside her.

As soon as I step in, our eyes connect. "Cal!" she screeches.

I'm not able to find time to process what is going on because that's when I see it. The gun.

Maggie. She's in the corner, arm shaking but still steady enough to aim. She's completely unhinged as sweat dampens the strands of hair plastered to her face.

"Drop the weapon," I bark, drawing my gun.

She spins toward me, eyes blazing.

"I said drop it," I repeat, low, controlled. "Don't make me ask again. You don't want to do this."

For a second—just a second—she falters. But then, in one swift motion, her aim swings back to Rose.

Pointing the gun right at her temple.

I take the shot.

The crack explodes through the room, sharp and deafening. Maggie screams, spinning as the bullet grazes her shoulder just as I intended. The gun slips from her grasp, clattering to the floor as she crumples beside it.

Rose and Diane cry out, their screams breaking into a mix of fear and relief.

Maggie clutches her arm, blood slick on her fingers as she cries in pain. "You ... you shot me."

Before I can react, there's motion behind me.

A blur.

Instinct kicks in. I whirl around, raising my gun.

Niko.

I was so focused on Maggie that I didn't even see him leave Rose's side. *Maybe I should have waited for back-up.*

Narrowing eyes snap to Rose, and I watch the realization slam into him. The betrayal, the shift, the way she clings to me with her gaze as if I'm the only safe thing in the room.

His expression curdles. "Liar!" he snarls. "You were *playing* me! You said we ... you promised ..."

"Niko, please." Rose's plea cracks, but it's too late.

He lunges.

I fire, but he's faster. He crashes into me, the force driving pain through my already wounded shoulder. My gun flies across the room. He lands a hard punch—once, twice—each blow turning the edges of my vision white. I grab his jacket, drive my knee into him, but I'm slower and weaker. He hits me again, this time splitting my eye open. I stumble, falling hard between the two beds, knocking the vintage alarm clock onto the floor. My head slams against the floor, stars bursting behind my eyes. The world tilts and fades.

Then goes black.

Again.

Chapter Twenty-Six
2:58 a.m.

Rose

Niko's roar tears through the room.

It's primal. Broken. Full of something I can't name.

Cal lies motionless by the bed, blood streaking down the side of his face. Maggie's on the floor too, one hand pressed against her shoulder, the other smeared red from trying to stop the bleeding. Her gun lies a few feet away, forgotten.

My pulse thrashes in my throat as I struggle against the ties cutting into my wrists. I look at Niko, wondering what is going to happen next as he stalks toward Maggie.

Oh, God, no. She might have caused all this pain, but she's still Maggie somewhere beneath the madness. And I can't let this happen. "Niko, please don't," I beg.

He doesn't hear me or even look at me. His eyes are locked on my cousin, wild and glassy. "You were going to kill her," he growls, stalking forward. "You were going to take her from me."

Maggie scrambles backward, the heels of her boots squealing against the floor. "Niko, wait—listen to me—" He pounces.

His hands wrap around her throat, and the sound that escapes her is half gasp, half scream. She claws at him, kicking, tears streaming down her face as she sputters, "Please—I didn't—"

"You were going to kill her!" he shouts, shaking her.

"Niko!" I cry, my voice raw. "Stop! Please, stop! This isn't you!"

Mom's sobbing from across the room, twisting against the ties binding her hands. "Niko, please!" she screams. "You'll kill her!"

But he doesn't stop. His knuckles are white as his face twists in pure rage and revenge.

Maggie's eyes start to roll back.

The air feels like it's shrinking, pressing down on me until I can't breathe either. I yank at the tie until it burns my skin, but it doesn't budge. "Niko, I'm begging you!"

The door slams open.

"Police! Drop her! Now!"

Denny's voice booms through the violence, his gun drawn, backup pouring in behind him.

Niko doesn't move. Doesn't even flinch. He just keeps whispering, over and over, "I love her. I love her. I love her." He's a man possessed.

"Let her go!" Denny yells, stepping closer, his tone cutting through the air like a crack of thunder.

Still nothing.

"Don't make me do this."

Slowly, Niko's grip falters.

He sucks in a long breath and releases her. Maggie collapses, gasping, her body shaking as she drags in air like it's the first breath she's ever taken.

For a long, endless second, the room is frozen.

Finally, movement.

Niko rises to his feet, and slowly lifts his palms in the air.

Surrendering.

He connects with me, eyes bloodshot and void of their usual blue sparkle. "*I'm sorry*," he mouths as he closes his eyes and bows his head.

The room erupts as officers rush in, shouting commands I can't make out.

Denny re-holsters his gun, runs to Niko, locking his arms behind his back, and gives him his Miranda Rights. "You have the right to remain silent. Anything you say can and will be…"

The room blurs into chaos as someone's cutting my ties, but I barely feel it. All I can do is stare. Niko's eyes flutter open, finding me through the haze. There's no rage there. Just regret. Denny ushers him out of the room.

And then he's gone.

The ties fall away, and I stumble to my feet. "Mom!" My knees give out halfway to her, and I collapse beside her chair. She's crying so hard she can't speak, her arms wrapping tight around me as soon as they're free, squeezing with the little strength she has left.

"It's over," I whisper, though my voice cracks on the words. "It's really over."

The rain outside has stopped, and for the first time in days, I let myself breathe.

And this time—it doesn't hurt.

Chapter Twenty-Seven

3:10 a.m.

Cal

"Cal." Her soft plea pulls me from the darkness. "Cal, please wake up."

It's as if my body is underwater. But she cuts through it all.

My Rose.

I blink hard as my vision swims into focus. The room's a blur of flashing red and blue lights from outside the window as people flood in and out of the room. The storm's finally breaking, but the commotion here hasn't.

"Hey," I rasp, my throat raw. She's crouched beside me. Her hands shake as she runs her fingers over my forehead.

Tears and weariness streak her glassy eyes. "You're okay," she breathes out with a tremble. "You're going to be okay."

Another familiar voice rumbles from somewhere behind her, barking orders at the uniforms flooding the room. Rose helps me sit upright as I wince in pain. I adjust myself against the mattress, leaning on it for support. I crane my neck over the bed, and Diane's being helped out of the chair, a blanket draped around her shoulders, paramedics doing their assessment. No doubt she will be on her way to the hospital soon.

I make a feeble attempt to stand, but pain flares through my shoulder and down my arm like fire. "AH!" I cry out through a chuckle. "Jesus Christ, this hurts."

Rose presses a hand against me, gentle but firm. "Don't you dare," she commands, her lip quivering. "You've lost too much blood."

"I'm fine," I insist. Because I will be. Now that we have each other.

She grins. "Liar."

I laugh, wincing through the pain. Leaning in, and as her tears fall onto my skin, Rose's soft lips find mine. It's tender, desperate, and full of the weight from the last few hours.

For a second, the rest of the world fades. The noise, the commotion, the storm—it all disappears.

It's just her. It's always only been her.

When she pulls back, I catch her face in my good hand. "Go," I flick my head. "Be with your mom."

"I don't want to leave you."

"Rose," I say, forcing a breath, "you've already done enough. Go." I implore softer now. "She needs you."

Tears spill over, but she nods, pressing her forehead to mine for another brief second before standing. I watch her walk away, and though I'm in the worst shape of my career, I've never felt more hopeful.

Denny crouches beside me, his expression tight. His jaw set. "Diane's safe," he says. "Maggie's in custody and on the way to the hospital." He pauses, glancing toward the open doorway where officers are still shouting commands down the hall.

"Why do I feel a 'but' coming on?" Heat rises to my head as I wait.

He sighs, wringing his hands. "But Niko," he pauses, then his lips curl into a teasing smile, "he's in custody."

I collapse against the bed in relief, laughing through the pain. "I hate it when you do that."

"You know me. I do that any chance I get. I love the panic on your face."

"Cute." I swallow. "Now fill me in."

"After he knocked you out, he decided to take his vengeance out on Maggie. He almost killed her. We got here just in time, and thankfully, he surrendered. Security and then Rose told us that he was the one who hacked into the hotel's system. He and Maggie were working together. It's a whole thing. I'll brief you at the hospital."

"So, it's over." Across the room, I find Rose, clutching her mother tightly, her body trembling with relief.

"It's over." He stands with purpose. "But now you are going to the hospital. No arguing."

I smile as I watch Rose adjust the blanket over her mom's shoulder.

Our eyes meet, and amidst all this hysteria, all I see is my future.

Chapter Twenty-Eight

3:43 a.m.

Rose

The storm has finally stopped.

Low moonlight seeps through the gray clouds, pale and weak after a night of thunder and mayhem. The smell of rain lingers as emergency lights flash against puddles of water.

Stepping out of the hotel's main entrance, the cool air pierces my face, and I tug the blanket the EMTs gave me around my body. Moments ago, I finished giving Denny a quick rundown of what happened in that room. He wants a full statement tomorrow, and Mom should be at the hospital soon.

We found her.

She's safe.

Right now, though, I can't stress about timelines or how the day played out. Because all I want is to find the man who saved my life.

Our lives.

Across the street, an ambulance sits with its back doors open, light spilling out onto the wet pavement. Cal's on a gurney with rain still clinging to his clothes. His shirt's torn open around his shoulder where blood seeps through fresh bandages. Paramedics move quickly around him, their commands clipped and urgent, but the moment he spots me, our eyes meet and hold.

And he smiles.

I dart across the intersection, my heart pounding. No matter how fast I move, it isn't quick enough.

Within seconds, I'm at his side. The sight of him steals my breath. His dark skin is ashen and almost gray from blood loss, with dark circles bruising his beautiful face.

But he's here.

He's alive.

And still so handsome.

"Ma'am, we're taking him in a few seconds," the paramedic says firm yet also kind.

Cal turns his head slightly. "Can you give us a minute?"

The paramedic hesitates, then nods, signaling the others to step back, and they scurry away.

And just like that, it's only us.

"Are you okay?" he inquires, loaded with concern. His hand finds mine, warm against the night chill.

Am I *okay*? This man took a bullet for me, and he's wondering if *I'm* okay.

"I should be asking you that," I joke, squeezing his hand gently.

He shrugs his good shoulder, a faint smile ghosting across his lips. "It's only a flesh wound."

I force a genuine, shaky laugh, tears welling up.

"That right there," he murmurs, his smile deepening. "That's what I wanted to hear."

The mood shifts, turning heavy again. "You saved us," I choke out.

The corners of his mouth tremble with exhaustion. "Well, getting shot wasn't part of the plan, but I'll take it." He pauses. "I'm so happy we found her."

My body just reacts—I bend down and kiss him. It's soft, quick, and full of every emotion coursing through me.

Gratitude.

Happiness.

Exhaustion.

Lust.

And the beginnings of love creeping in.

As I pull back, his knuckles brush against my cheek, both rough and surprisingly gentle.

"Guess that's your way of saying thank you," he says on exhale.

I grin. "Something like that."

"We really have to get going." The paramedics move to load him into the ambulance, but he grabs my hand before they can roll him away.

"I would love a repeat of that night," he says without elaborating. I grin, knowing exactly what night he's referring to.

The night he left me confused on the sidewalk after our amazing date at the bar.

The night he almost kissed me and then bolted.

The night Cal says he regrets more than anything.

The night Niko showed up.

I snicker, even as my eyes sting. "You're really asking me out right now?"

"Timing's everything," he says with a tired grin.

"Of course," I answer. "But we will make it better this time."

"Oh, absolutely." His thumb grazes my palm before he lets go and they lift him into the back of the ambulance. He winks. "I'll see you soon, Sheridan."

"Wait!" I call out, cutting through the noise as the EMT reaches for the door. I'm not ready to let him go.

Not quite yet.

Before anyone can stop me, I climb into the rig and reach for him. Our lips meet for a final time before the healing begins. When we pull apart, I cradle his face in my hands, my thumb tracing the rough edge of his jaw.

"The storm we breathe," I whisper, the words trembling but sure. The same ones on the neon light in his office. A promise of survival, and love.

Us.

His gaze locks with mine, a faint smile curving his lips. "The storm we breathe," he murmurs.

We're holding on tight to this moment, too afraid to let go.

"Ma'am, we can't wait anymore." The EMT's words break us from our love haze.

One last peck then I hop out of the rig and the doors close. I watch and yearn as the ambulance pulls away with the sirens echoing faintly in the distance.

Denny stands nearby, talking quietly with officers and hotel security. I cross the street again, and when he sees me, his face softens. "He's going to be okay."

"I know. I just—" I lower my head, tugging the blanket tighter.

"Just what?" he asks, leaning, concerned.

"I just realized I don't have his personal number."

Denny throws his head back and lets out a deep, hearty laugh. "I can fix that. Only ever gave you the work cell, huh?"

I nod, smiling.

He chuckles, shaking his head. "That Cal. Always so professional." Denny offers me a warm smile. "I'll make sure you get that."

As soon as I have that number, I know exactly what I'm going to do with it. "Thank you."

"Is your car in the garage?" he asks. "I'll walk you there."

A rush of relief washes through me. "Yes, please. I don't think I will ever look at a parking garage the same way again."

We fall into a quiet stride, neither of us rushing to fill the silence, leaving the chaos behind us. "Your mom's stable," he says after a moment. "She's going to be all right."

That's when it hits me. Hearing that all my loved ones are now safe nearly knocks the breath out of me. I press a hand to my stomach and nod. "I know."

He studies my face for a beat, then says softly, "You did good tonight, Rose."

"Thank you," I reply through a tight smile, not completely convinced as my thoughts drift to the mastermind of this whole thing. "What happens to Maggie?"

Denny's jaw tightens as we turn toward the garage. "Well, she has been arrested and is on her way to the prisoners' wing of the hospital. As soon as she's stable, she will be transferred to county. After that, depending on what she's charged with and pleads, well, that will determine her future."

"Which I'm sure will be jail time."

"Yes, more than likely."

He stops and sets a hand on my shoulder, firm and steady. "Now it's time to rebuild your life. And for you and your mom to heal." I nod. "You sure you want to give Cal a chance? He can be a handful."

We both laugh. "Yes. I do. More than anything."

6:41 a.m.

Hours later, at the hospital, I sit at Mom's bedside and watch her drift into sleep. The first appearance of morning streams in through the window. Steady beeps of the monitors fill the silence. A rhythm I can finally trust. She's alive. She's here. That's all that matters.

Mom kept insisting I go home, but I couldn't bring myself to leave. So, I called my neighbor to let out Juno as I pulled up a chair next to her bed.

Mom was having a hard time sleeping, despite her exhaustion. The doctor finally gave her something to help her rest, and when her breathing evens out into soft, steady snores, I smile. That sound is the most comforting thing I've heard in days.

I rise quietly and kiss her forehead. "I'll be back in a few hours, Mom," I promise.

God, I can't wait to go home and take a long, hot bath, sleep, curl up with Juno, and call Cal.

Denny did give me his number, after all.

As I step into the hallway, fatigue catches up with me, but something else does too.

A thought.

A pull.

A need.

When I spot Denny down the hall talking with an officer, I draw in a deep breath and make my way toward him. He sees me, offering a small, tired smile. I'm sure he's been awake for over twenty-four hours.

"I want to talk to her," I demand, steadier than I appear.

His smile fades. He doesn't ask who I mean. He already knows. "Maggie's in police custody," he retorts. "She's under guard."

"Please," I beg quietly. "It will only take a few minutes."

He studies me for a long moment before agreeing. "You get five. I'll take you there."

Two floors higher now, and this area of the hospital is colder, less friendly. The hallway grows more sterile the farther we go. When we reach the guarded door, two armed officers stand outside, arms crossed, their expressions like stone. When they see Denny, they both offer a single nod.

I peek through the narrow window.

Maggie sits semi-upright in the hospital bed. Her arm is in a sling, while a cuff secures the hand of her good arm to the bed. A brace is wrapped around her neck while a stiff white blanket covers her legs. Her normally perfect hair is a complete mess. She's staring out the window, and her face is lit by the light of morning.

A sharp ache cuts through me. She's a stranger now, nothing like the friend and cousin I grew up with. When did everything fall apart? How did we get so lost? And how was I so blind?

I shake these thoughts free and square my shoulders. Plus, the therapy needed to address these questions is going to cost me a fortune. *Thanks, Maggie.*

"She's stable," Denny says gently, the edge gone from his voice. "Cal's aim is always perfect. The bullet only grazed her shoulder. He wasn't trying to kill her, just stop her." He pauses, watching my reaction before continuing, "We'll be transferring her to county soon."

Good. I do not want her in the same building as my mom.

He steps a little closer, lowering his voice. "Do you want me to go in with you?" he asks, quiet but steady, like he's ready to shield me from whatever's waiting on the other side of that door.

I'm still staring through the glass. "No. I'll be okay."

"I'll be right here." He opens the door for me.

Maggie's head jerks toward the sound. The moment she sees me, her shallow expression hardens, sharpening like glass.

"Come to gloat?" she rasps, her voice hoarse from Niko's strength.

I step inside, closing the door behind me. "No. I just ..." My thoughts falter. I hadn't thought this through. "In a weird way, I wanted to make sure you're okay." It's true. Why? I don't know, really. When I look at her, I see my Maggie. But then, I remember.

Her lips twist. "How generous of you."

I swallow hard, trying to steady myself. "You threw your life away, Maggie. You could've had so much—love, friends, a future that actually meant something. But you chose this instead … to hurt us. *Kill us.* And for what?"

Her eyes flash as she trembles with rage. "Don't you dare pretend you care about me! You took everything, Rose! You always did. All the attention, friends, even Niko's love. And now, you have Cal." Her voice cracks. "You think I could stand there and watch you have what I never did?"

"I didn't take anything from you," I respond softly. As mad as I am, I won't stoop to her level of bitterness and hate. "You couldn't see that no one was keeping it from you either."

She stares at me for a long moment, her breathing uneven. Then she looks away. "I hate you," she murmurs. "Always have. I always will." Her attention snaps back to me, sharp like daggers. "God, do you know what a relief it is to say that? Not to pretend anymore and act fake. Act as if I loved you." She rolls her eyes. "It's so liberating, you know? Keeping up that act was *exhausting,* let me tell you."

With a single nod, something inside me settles. An unexpected calm.

Maggie is gone. Whoever she used to be … she's not coming back. I'm not sure she ever existed to begin with. And accepting that might be the only way I survive this. The only way I move on.

"Good," I say quietly, meeting her stare. "I'm glad you finally stopped pretending."

Her nostrils flare, anger sparking hard and fast, but I push on before she can twist it into something else.

"And don't worry about faking anything anymore," I add low and steady. "You won't ever have to see me again."

I walk toward the door, then glance back one last time. "Enjoy prison, Maggie."

Her laugh is low and humorless. "Enjoy your perfect life. While it lasts."

I walk out before she can say another word. And I leave her behind. Forever.

Denny is waiting in the hall, arms crossed, his expression soft with something akin to pride. "She's not worth another thought," he says gently. "You've been through enough."

Maybe he's right. Maybe it's time to stop replaying the what–ifs and start believing in what's next.

"Go home. Get some rest. We'll be in touch." Without thinking, I go in for a hug. "Woah," he stumbles back from the embrace. Then, he wraps his arms around me.

"Thank you," I mumble into his chest. "For everything."

When I step outside, the early morning air is cool and clean, washing away the weight of everything that's happened. And as I look up, the clouds are finally breaking, revealing the first trace of morning light.

Epilogue

Eighteen months later

Rose

The lights strung on the rooftop terrace sway gently in the evening breeze and glow like stars against the soft city skyline. Music hums from hidden speakers, laughter surrounds us, and even though it's been a while, I feel light again.

It's my book release party.

The first copies of *Fear Will Become Us* sit stacked on a small table near the bar, their glossy covers catching the light. Writing this book is what brought Cal into my life. His influence seeps into each page.

However, my name looks strange on the front, like it belongs to someone else. It was almost surreal. Because so much has happened since I penned these words. I'm a different person now.

Hmm, maybe I'll start writing under a pen name.

Focusing on the future is a really good feeling.

After that fateful night, the police arrested Maggie (obviously) and charged her with a laundry list of crimes. She pled guilty, and the judge sentenced her to fifteen to twenty years. She's serving out her time in a prison four hours away.

I haven't spoken to her since that day at the hospital. Mom, Denny, Cal, and I did, however, attend her sentencing hearing. The court asked whether we wanted to make a statement.

We both refused.

Then there's Niko. He pleaded not guilty, and the trial dragged on for two long weeks. His weak and lame defense was that Maggie forced him into everything. We were all subpoenaed to testify, which was ... brutal. Reliving everything that happened felt like tearing open wounds that were just starting to heal. But if it meant justice, if it meant making sure he could never hurt anyone again, it was worth it.

Maggie had to testify also. Seeing her in person—hearing her testify about the events—was hard enough. But listening as she laid out, for the first time, how they planned everything from the start made it worse. There was no remorse in her voice. No awareness of the damage she'd caused. If anything, it was proof she hadn't learned a single thing from her mistakes.

When her testimony ended and she was escorted out of the courtroom, she turned back and flipped us off as a final goodbye.

Thankfully, the jury saw the truth, and they found him guilty on all charges. His sentencing is next week, and I can only hope the judge throws the book at him. Maybe then, we can all officially move on.

Mom is standing near the railing, a glass of champagne in her hand, appearing healthier than I've seen her in months. Both of us are in therapy, trying to process and heal. Maggie's betrayal, the lies, and for me, Niko.

All of it.

Our typical brush-it-off mentality wasn't working like it had before. This was too big. Too hard. So the therapy's been helpful. It's been difficult to navigate. Maggie was a big part of my life, which now makes my happy childhood memories tainted.

Processing it all has been my biggest challenge, but I'm moving on.

My mom, though, has dealt with some depression and anxiety stemming from all the trauma. She's managing it, and lately, it's like the fog is lifting.

She's smiling again. And finding joy in her job and life.

And through it all, my rock, my gorgeous boyfriend, stands beside me. Like he is right now.

It was a few months before we actually got around to that drink. Cal's shoulder surgery kept him grounded for a while, and recovery wasn't exactly romantic. But we made the best of it. There were long nights, slow progress, and laughter where we could find it. It was during this time, though, that we really got to know each other, which only brought us closer.

We joke about how we were technically together that whole time but couldn't have a proper date. When we finally did, though, it definitely made up for the last attempt.

Right now, Cal's dressed in a crisp white shirt and a light gray jacket with matching slacks that hug his legs. The change suits him. It's subtle and understated. Just like Cal. He even has a little color in his wardrobe now.

Yeah, okay … it's only gray and white. I can't push too hard.

I spot one of Juno's hairs clinging to Cal's forearm and try to pluck it off before he notices.

He notices. He always does. "That little guy follows me everywhere, doesn't he?" he quips through a smirk.

I flick the hair away and squeeze his arm. "He's claimed you," I tease.

It's true … Juno completely won him over. At first, Cal swore he wasn't a small dog guy, always insisting he preferred big, tough dogs like German Shepherds or Labs. Then, one afternoon during his recovery, Juno climbed into his lap, gave him one lick on the hand, and that was it. Instant best friends.

Now, the two best men in my life are inseparable. Honestly, what more could I ask for?

Cal grins, glancing at me and playfully nudging my side. "Well," he says, "you could ask him to stop stealing my favorite chair."

I laugh. "Not a chance. He was there first."

He chuckles, amused. "Figures. Guess I'll have to share my girl with a dog."

The breeze lifts a stray curl from my forehead, and his eyes track the motion, soft and full of something that makes my heart stutter.

I love these two sides of Cal. The tough cop and the tender loving man that's here tonight. Both versions stir my blood.

"You did it," Cal says quietly, his hand brushing mine.

I grin. "We did it." He kisses me gently. "Seriously, I couldn't do any of this without you and your support."

He places a soft peck at the end of my nose. "You'll always have my support, Sheridan." I love that he still calls me that. I'm Rose when it counts. Those private, quiet moments when it's just us, and I'm nuzzled up against him. But when we are outside of that, I'm Sheridan.

He tilts his head. "So what's next for the great Rose Sheridan?"

I sip my champagne, eyes glinting. "Actually … after some thought, I think my next book's going to be about what happened. All of it."

He rears his body back and chuckles. "Really? You didn't tell me that. Nonfiction?"

"Fictionalized," I say with a smirk. "Names changed, events re-arranged. But the truth will still be there."

He nods thoughtfully. "You're braver than most."

"You're braver than them all."

Across the terrace, Denny appears next to my mom, his tie slightly loosened, the ever-serious broody detective looking oddly relaxed.

When Cal requested the night off for the party, Denny's reply was everything and more. "Of course. So what time should I be there, and do I have to wear a tie?" When Cal told me, I had to negotiate an extra ticket for him. I love that he fits right in with our crazy group. I wouldn't change a thing.

And the other person I had to fenagle a ticket for is walking toward us. The head of security. Michael Hawkins. After everything, he approached Denny and asked him if the precinct had any job openings. Turns out the failings of the hotel was his last straw. He had been ready to move on for a while, tired of their incompetence. Plus, he forgot how much he loved detective work. And since Cal was so impressed with him, the decision was an easy one.

He was hired in two months later. And is now one of Cal's best friends.

"I just wanted to come over and say bye," he offers, warm as always. "Congratulations Rose."

"Thanks Michael." I smile at the man that helped more then he knows that night.

He slaps Cal on the arm. "Poker at my place tomorrow?"

"I'll be there." Cal says with a laugh.

Michael jerks his head in the direction of my mom. "Well, I would say good-bye to Denny but he looks a little busy," he says with a wink as he walks away.

My eyes dart back to the railing and Denny rests his elbows on the glass by Mom, then leans in to say something. She laughs. A real, unguarded laugh that I haven't heard from her in a very long time.

Cal follows my line of sight and grins. "Well, well."

I nudge him with my elbow. "What?"

"Your mom and my boss," he says, raising an eyebrow and then taking another pull of his drink.

"I definitely saw that coming." I laugh softly. With all the trial prep, the four of us have spent plenty of time together. It was in those moments that my mom would light up.

And I knew why.

Cal leans in and whispers in my ear, "If he offers to buy her a drink, we might be in trouble."

At that exact moment, Denny mouths something and gestures toward the bar. Mom blushes, smiles, and follows him.

Cal snorts. "Called it."

"I love it." I laugh, nodding my head.

We watch them go, both of us smiling. My mom and Denny. Somehow, it fits. Seeing her laugh again is amazing. To know that the storm has passed.

"So," I say, placing my drink on a neighboring table, then turning to him, resting my palms on his shirt, "what do you have planned for later?"

He slides his arm around my waist, pulling me just close enough to make my breath catch. "It's a surprise," he murmurs.

I tilt my head, pretending to pout. "You know I hate surprises."

He kisses me softly, the kind of kiss that still makes me giddy no matter how many times he's done it. "You'll like this one," he promises against my lips. "I have a question to ask you."

We exchange a knowing, lingering look as I raise an eyebrow. His lips press against my forehead. "Nevermind, I'm not waiting anymore. Let's get out of here."

I glance around the open space, content with the evening. "I think I've schmoozed enough people."

Cal slings his arm around my shoulder and we walk toward the elevator, the laughter and music fading behind us. As the doors slide shut, I spin, grab his jacket collar, and pull his lips to mine.

You know, since we're big on elevator kisses.

It's kind of our thing.

The Storm We Breathe

Playlist

- The One That Got Away – **The Civil Wars**

- Black – **Kari Kimmel**

- Lonely Boy – **The Black Keys**

- Sorry – **NF, James Arthur**

- Secrets – **OneRepublic**

- If You Were Mine – **Morgan Wallen**

- With Or Without You – **U2**

- November Rain – **Guns N' Roses**

- These Arms of Mine – **Otis Redding**

- Faster – **Matt Nathanson**

- Lose Myself – **Lera Lynn, John Paul White**

- Death Wish Love – **Benson Boone**

- Amazing – **Teddy Swims**

- Sweet Child O' Mine – **Guns N' Ros**es

- #1 Crush – **Garbage**

- Look What You Made Me Do – **Taylor Swift**

- In The Air Tonight – **Phil Collins**

- Uninvited – **Alanis Morissette**

- Carry You Home – **Alex Warren**

- iris – **mgk, Julia Wolf**

- Opalite – **Taylor Swift**

Acknowledgements

Before this book became the version you just finished reading, it had a completely different identity. There was a time traveling elevator, neon signs (big ones!), a cover concept that got lost in translation (it was WILD), and an ending that, as my son worded it, was very Lifetime Movie. His exact words were, "Oh my God Mom, please get rid of that." Looking back now, he wasn't wrong. LOL!

Well, needless to say, lots of changes needed to be made. So thank you to my Beta readers and critique partners, Delaney, my husband Brian, my daughter Samantha, and my son Jackson. This book is what it is because of your honesty! All of your ideas and criticisms were exactly what this book needed. It's better, and a true romantic suspense because of all of you. I know it's all done out of love.

Thank you once again to my editor Nevvie. I should include you in the above group because you saw some little inconsistencies that needed addressed. Thank goodness! You are worth your weight in gold!

And of course, I need to thank you, my readers. I decided to take a risk with this book and write something that was completely out of my comfort zone. It was a challenge and honestly, it about killed me. So, I can't thank you enough for taking a chance and reading it. I truly hope you enjoyed it and that you will stick around for more. Because this author has many more tricks up her sleeve!

About the author

Elaine Evans has had a love of writing ever since she can remember. But it wasn't until she hit middle age that she turned it into a second career. The Storm We Breathe is her fourth novel.

When she isn't writing or working at her day job (a medical assistant at a children's hospital), you can find Elaine pursuing her other hobbies and interests. She loves cooking, baking, photography, and, of course, reading. In the fall and winter, you will find her on Sunday's rooting for the Pittsburgh Steelers. But it's her role as wife, mother, and dog mom to her Pomeranian Vinnie, that brings her the most joy.

Elaine would love to connect with her readers! You can find her on Instagram, Facebook, and Goodreads.

instagram.com/elaineevanswrites

goodreads.com/author/show/1739279.Elaine_Evans

facebook.com/profile.php?id=61557583049180